# Swept Off my Feet

## INES BAUTISTA-YAO

*To Corinne,*

*thank you for being my inspiration and for always supporting me. I hope you find your happily ever after too.*

# *Chapter 1*

◁

This wasn't the plan. I wasn't supposed to be dragging my worn-out backpack across the wooden floor of this dark, stuffy studio that smelled like sweaty feet. I was supposed to be in our regular ballet studio with its warm, vanilla fragrance wafting from Teacher Justine's scented candles. Sadly, it had a leaky roof and we couldn't exactly do our twirls and pliés surrounded by buckets of water waiting to collect excess rain. And monsoon weather in Metro Manila meant lots and lots of excess rain.

So there I was inhaling stinky feet, which, I had to admit, I was used to. I play basketball and the smell of feet is something you build a tolerance for pretty quickly. But today, I wasn't going to play ball. I was here to dance.

I plopped down on the floor nearest the mirror that spanned an entire wall from floor to ceiling. Turning my back to it, I slid my basketball into a corner and began to unlace my sneakers. It was time to morph from sporty Geri into the ballerina my heart desperately craved to be. I blew my bangs out of my eyes and secured my short hair with a terry cloth headband. Yeah, I know. Way to be graceful. But that was all I had. It wasn't like I could spend my allowance on girly hair accessories.

I pulled my soft, pink ballet shoes from my backpack, cradled them in my hands for a few seconds, and was about to slip them on when I heard the doorknob turn. My eyes narrowed as I tried to focus on the figure stepping through. He was wearing what looked like a white martial arts kimono over a dark colored tee. He lifted his arm toward the light switch and the room was flooded in bright, white light.

"Who are you?" we asked at the same time.

I didn't like the way he was frowning at me. And towering over me. I leapt to my feet. "I reserved the studio for our ballet class."

He strode over to where I stood and dropped his dirty-looking backpack with a thud. "Well, every afternoon, the *dojo*," he stressed on the word, "is ours."

I looked around the empty room, noticing the blue mats stacked against one corner. Oh, right. There they were. But I couldn't resist saying, "Doesn't look like much of a dojo to me."

"I'm here to set up the mats," he muttered, giving me a stern look before marching over to them.

"Wait a minute!" I realized he wasn't going to listen to me. "We're here to dance and we can't exactly do pirouettes on mats."

"Didn't you hear what I said? This *dojo*," he paused and I tried really hard not to stick my tongue out at him, "is reserved."

My hands flew to my hips, landing on the waistband of my basketball shorts. "I reserved this studio for the rest of the month. Our ballet studio has a leak—"

"I don't care about your leak. You can't have the dojo because I reserved it."

That was it. Who did he think he was, throwing his weight around like this? "Look," I spat out. "All we have to do is check with the secretary who will tell you that *you*," I emphasized, "made a mistake."

"I did not make a mistake." He grabbed one of the mats and tossed it on the floor. I was about to walk over and put it back against the wall, but I figured that would be a waste of time. Besides, Teacher Justine and the rest of my classmates were going to be here in a few minutes and I still hadn't set up the speakers or the rosin for our pointe shoes.

"Well, neither did I." I pushed both hands against the door and stomped through the narrow hallway to the administration office. Well, I tried to stomp but couldn't actually manage it in my soft ballet shoes. Padded was a more appropriate term.

I knocked on the pale wooden door and didn't wait for an invitation to enter. "Ms. Sue," I began as she peered up from her cluttered desk. "There's this guy saying the studio is reserved for—"

"The *dojo*."

I spun around and jumped back when I discovered he was standing right behind me in the cramped office. I didn't want to be closer to him than I had to be. And being in the same spacious studio was already more than I could take. I banged my butt against Ms. Sue's desk, pitching a few papers to the floor, and yelped.

I glared at him when he snickered. Ms. Sue, however, was already next to me, her hand on my waist, asking if I was okay.

"I thought you said you were a ballet dancer." He smirked.

"What's that supposed to mean?" That stung a little bit.

"Well, aren't ballerinas supposed to be graceful? That wasn't exactly an act of grace." As the corner of his lip curled upwards, I gripped the edge of Ms. Sue's desk to keep my hands from grabbing something, like her glass paperweight, and hurling it at his smug face.

Ms. Sue raised both hands and waved them in our faces. She was tiny, maybe not even five feet, and she looked even smaller next to him. It was then that I noticed how tall he was.

The guys I met were usually around my height, which was four inches below six feet. But to look at his annoying smirk, I had to bend my neck back a bit. "I'm so sorry, Bas," she began in her high-pitched voice. "Geri is right. The studio is hers at this time. Didn't Sensei tell you?"

He bent his head and shoulders in what looked like a bow. This guy really internalized his costume, didn't he?

"Thank you, Ms. Sue. No, he didn't." He gave me a tight smile. "Sorry about that." And turned away.

That was it? And to think I was ready to fight. I stood there watching him walk back to the studio when I felt Ms. Sue tap me on the back. "He's really a sweetheart. Just very passionate about aikido."

I shook my head and turned to thank her. I made sure to confirm that I had reserved the studio every weekday afternoon and every Saturday morning for a month so I wouldn't get into more trouble with Dojo guy, then I jogged back to get the stuff ready. When I arrived at the dojo, uh, I mean studio, the mat he had put on the floor was already against the wall and he was nowhere to be found. I didn't bother to check if he was hanging around outside to thank him for doing that. By then, I had lost precious minutes arguing over the legitimacy of my reservation.

I tugged off my shorts and tied my delicate, pink skirt around my waist. I was already wearing my pink tights and black leotard underneath my basketball clothes. I pulled at my hair, hoping today would be the day I could finally tie it into a ponytail, but no such luck. I had to make do with the headband. I was growing my hair out because really, have you seen a shorthaired ballerina? Short hair worked when you played ball. Once during practice, someone yanked my ponytail hard while I was trying to do a layup. It hurt so much, tears stung my eyes. That was when I decided it was not going to happen again. So off to the barber's I went.

But when Teacher Justine came to school two years ago to take over my freshman P.E. class, forcing us to do what she called layman ballet, I felt like I had tasted ice cream for the very first time. The same arms I used to tap the ball in an attempt to steal could extend above my head in a graceful arc. The same feet I pumped across the court to make a basket could go on tiptoe and lift me up. I surprised myself by chasing after Teacher Justine when P.E. ended and begging her to let me know how I could enroll in her class.

"You're older than the usual starting age, but you have great proportions, Geri Lazaro." Those words were like an ice-cold bottle of Gatorade after realizing I'd forgotten my water jug halfway through basketball practice. Thus the terrycloth headband and the dream of getting hair extensions.

"Did you see him?" My ballet classmate Helena, whose hair was always in a perfect bun without a single strand out of place, floated over to me, pink skirts flapping up and down in her rush.

"Who?"

"This guy! I can't believe you didn't see him!" She held her phone out toward me. Then her bright, excited expression fell. "Oh, Geri, I hope you weren't wearing your basketball outfit when you arrived."

I pulled her phone closer so I could study the image on it. I blinked when I saw who it was: Dojo guy. He was talking to someone else in a martial arts kimono. A girl with long hair cascading down her back. So there was no question of who Helena had just stalked in that photo. I put Helena's phone back in her hand and wrinkled my nose. "Ew. Yeah. We kinda got into an argument." I saw her eyes widen. "And yeah, I was wearing my basketball clothes."

"Geri!" She raised both hands. Even in her frustration, she did it with such grace. No wonder she was Teacher Justine's star pupil. "What on earth did you argue about?"

She started pressing something on her phone. In a few seconds, I heard mine beep in the depths of my backpack. I had to remember to put it on silent during class. "Did you just send me his photo? I don't want it."

"So delete it." She grinned, a teasing look in her dark, round eyes. "Why were you fighting?"

I walked toward the power outlet to plug in Teacher Justine's portable speakers. "He was insisting that the studio belonged to him at this time. But I sorted it out with the admin secretary."

"That doesn't sound like something you have to fight over." She tilted her pretty head to the side, her gentle voice a perfect match to her fluid movements. "Is it because you have issues with cute guys?"

I gaped at her. "What do you mean? I do not have issues with cute guys."

"Yes you do. You can't stand your mom's boyfriend. He's gorgeous." Helena's hands flew to her tiny waist.

I reached for the remote control of the air-conditioner, which hung on the wall, and pressed the green button. As cool air began to permeate the room, I turned to face her. "My mom's boyfriend is not gorgeous. Stop being gross, Helena."

"Maybe if you weren't in those horrible basketball clothes, you wouldn't have been so combative," she countered.

"Combative?"

Helena nodded. "Sorry, hon, but you get a bit aggressive when you're in them. Why do you still wear them? It's not like you attend training anymore, right?" Her brow furrowed as if she were trying to understand the complications of my challenged wardrobe.

"I still do! It's not basketball season though, so Coach lets me leave earlier to make it to ballet on time. Since I can't exactly walk around in just my ballet clothes, I put my shorts and jersey over them for the trip here."

"Are you sure about this, Geri?" Helena bit her lower lip. "Have you ever considered ditching basketball? Are you truly planning to make a career out of it?"

"Hey, the Philippine Basketball Association is starting a women's league!" I protested. But I knew it was useless. Helena didn't care about sports. I think the only time she ever watched basketball was whenever I had a game, and afterwards, she'd keep asking me why this or that happened. It was tiring but I was grateful for her support.

I got down on the floor and extended my legs into a good stretch, hoping that would get her mind off my sport *and* Dojo guy.

It worked.

"Oh, Geri, if you angle your leg like this, you'll get an even more satisfying stretch." She floated down next to me to get into the position.

When I first started, Teacher Justine assigned her to help me catch up. I still had a long way to go, but Helena, who had been dancing ever since she could pull her ballet shoes on her tiny chubby feet at two-and-a-half, was the most patient teacher ever. She was just a pest when it came to boys. And other things too. It was like she had an agenda to make over my life together with my dancing skills.

"Good afternoon, girls." We looked up to see Teacher Justine glide into the room. Behind her were the rest of our classmates.

I scrambled to my feet and we curtseyed together. I swear, it wasn't planned, but the proud smile on Helena's face told me it was now going to be our standard greeting whenever Teacher Justine entered the studio.

Teacher Justine stood in the center, right next to the mirrored wall, her heels together and her toes pointing outward in classic ballet first position. I don't think she was even aware she was doing it. Her tummy was tucked in and her back was ramrod straight. She sniffed the air and turned her head as if searching for someone. "Geri," she began. I stood up straighter. "Please take the candles from that paper bag and light them. I don't know how we can dance with this smell."

I curtseyed again and tried my best to be light on my feet as I rushed to retrieve the candles and return to my spot in front of Teacher Justine. We were only seven in class, so there was no way I could hide behind Helena. But then again, I wanted to do this. I wanted to be a ballerina.

It wasn't because of the flouncy skirts, elaborate costumes, studded tiaras, or even the satiny, pointe shoes. It was how I felt when I was moving my body to the music: strong, powerful, in control—yet not. As if something more graceful was powering through me and I was a conduit, a channel for all this movement. As I danced, I felt as if everything was right in the world—as if I was doing what I was born to do. It wasn't like that on the basketball court. Sure, I loved the rush, the adrenaline, the bond with my team, even the sweat that cooled me down after a hard drive, but it wasn't anything like this.

I concentrated on tucking my tummy in just a little bit tighter and holding myself up just a little bit straighter as I extended my arms on either side of me. Each miniscule movement had to be precise, controlled. I could feel the beads of sweat form on my nose and I was dying to rub them off, but as Helena says, "Always dance as if you were onstage." When Teacher Justine inclined her head in approval as she drifted by me, I felt my heart lift. It didn't matter where we were dancing—smelly studio complete with annoying Dojo guy or a brightly lit stage with hundreds in the audience. What mattered was that we were dancing—that I was dancing.

# Chapter 2

I caught a ride home with Helena after class because Mom called to say she had to stay late at work. In the car, Helena kept talking about Dojo guy. I didn't understand what the fuss was about. Was it because he was tall? And not scrawny? I did notice that his kimono thing didn't hang loosely off his shoulders. He looked...solid. I guess that's the word I'd use to describe him. Makes him sound like a building. Tall and solid.

And annoying. Definitely annoying.

"I'd put up with annoying if he were that cute." Helena sighed.

I didn't bother to answer. I knew it was an argument I would lose anyway. Besides, we were already pulling up alongside my house.

"See you in ballet class tomorrow, Geri!" Helena enveloped me in a hug. Her driver was already holding the door open for me when I turned to let myself out of the plush, air-conditioned comfort of the luxury vehicle. I tugged my backpack off the carpeted floor and cradled my basketball in my left arm. The moment I stepped out of the car, I felt the coolness on my skin evaporate in the late afternoon humidity.

"Thanks again, Helena. *Salamat*, Kuya Dex." I stood in front of my front lawn and watched the sleek, black car drive away.

Our house was one of the few in the village that didn't have a gate. Mom inherited it when Lola Sony, her unmarried grandaunt, passed away. When Mom got pregnant with me, Lola Sony invited her to move in. She had taken Mom aside while she was crying her eyes out, fresh from the humiliation of telling her parents she'd missed her period and tested positive on an early pregnancy test. "*Hija*, you can live with me and ask that nice boy John to move in with us when the baby's born. I believe that little one will need both parents under one roof, don't you?"

I remember Mom telling me that she couldn't believe her ears. She'd thrown her arms around Lola Sony and despite the protests of her parents, made a life with Dad and me. When Lola Sony passed away a few years after I was born, they didn't bother to look for another place to live. They never got around to getting married either, for whatever reason. Maybe that was why Dad thought he could just up and leave.

I rang the doorbell, waiting for Yaya Agnes to open the door. I was surprised when it swung back to reveal not the small, cushiony softness of my *yaya* who had started out as Lola Sony's household help, but the sturdy torso of someone who was unquestionably of the male gender.

"Oh, it's you." I pushed my way through, grimacing as my shoulder bumped against his chest. It wouldn't have if he'd just moved aside like a normal person.

"Hi, Geri!" I allowed myself to glance up at him and his irritatingly big smile. *Trying too hard, Matt. You're always trying too hard with me.* "Do you want to join me? I made a few sandwiches and am about to marathon *Star Trek Voyager*."

"No thanks." And of course my stomach just had to let out a growl. An audible one.

"Sounds like you want one." He laughed. "Don't worry, they're not poisoned." He shut the door and sauntered over to the long, cream-colored couch in our living room. When Dad moved out, Mom remodeled and threw out Lola Sony's old furniture. She spent money she didn't have on couches, side tables, chairs, and lamps in neutral colors. Then she went wild on throw pillows, bright colored picture frames, and prints for the walls. I had to admit the pops of color and decorative accents were interesting and made our home feel even more inviting. But seeing her boyfriend on our pretty couch, munching on a ham and cheese sandwich that he made in our cozy kitchen, most probably with the help of my doting Yaya Agnes, made my stomach turn.

"I don't like ham and cheese." A flat-out lie. But I refused to sit next to him and get all chummy. Matt had managed to worm his way into everyone's heart—Yaya Agnes's, my grandparents', even my friends', but he was not going to win me over. No way. I had a dad. I didn't need a new one. Besides, Matt was closer to my age than he was to Mom's. Okay maybe that wasn't exactly on point. He was what, twenty-nine? And Mom was almost forty. I was against this relationship from the start.

"Come on, Ger. You love this show. Your mom said—"

"I'm tired. Just came from ballet class, Matt. I'm going upstairs to lie down. I guess you're waiting till Mom comes home?" As much as I couldn't stand him, he made Mom happy. So happy. And I hated that it repulsed me.

"I wanted to take you guys out tonight. It's our anniversary. But your mom had to work late." He put the show on pause and looked up at me.

I wrinkled my nose. "And why aren't you at work?" I know, I know. I should have just stopped talking to him and gone upstairs, but really, I couldn't resist making him feel like an irresponsible freeloader.

"I come in earlier now so I can leave earlier too. Gives me more time to do other things outside the office. Besides, today is a special day." He smiled. I noticed for what seemed like the millionth time how white and straight his teeth were. It made me wonder if Mom sometimes felt the pressure to look younger than her age because she was dating Matt. I guess it helped that she was small, a lot shorter than me, and she did look young. Especially for someone who had a sixteen-year-old daughter.

I breathed out. "I hope she comes home soon and you guys can still head out. I have homework." I turned away before I could catch the disappointment in his eyes. Ever since he entered our lives two years ago, that was the look my words inspired. I made sure of it.

When I got to my room at the top of the stairs, I dropped my backpack on the floor and sank onto my bed to tug off my basketball shoes. I began to gently roll off my once-black-now-graying socks, grimacing at how baggy they'd gotten around my ankles. I found them inside the bag Dad used to take whenever he played ball on Tuesday nights. He forgot to bring it with him in his haste to leave. Or maybe he didn't want to take it. Since he was starting a new life and all. Without us. Without me.

His bag's dark blue material was fraying at the seams, the leather strap was crumbling, and the inside smelled like musty, unwashed sports jerseys. When I spotted it that night in his closet, seven years ago, a few nights after he'd left, I tucked it under my arm and spirited it into my room. I hid it underneath my bed, behind three dusty, stuffed bears he had given me for my fifth birthday. I shoved them there because I was afraid Mom would throw them out the way she did everything else that belonged to him, everything else he had given her. Eleven years later, the bears were still there but not because I was afraid Mom would throw them out anymore. I liked having them near me when I went to sleep. Protecting me from any monsters that lived under my bed. Something my daddy would have done had he hung around longer.

You could say the right corner of my room, next to my bed, was a sort of tribute to him. On the wall, next to my glass window was a six-foot-tall poster of Michael Jordan, in his white Chicago Bulls uniform, mouth wide open, right arm extended, about to make a slam dunk. Dad said it used to hang in his room when he was in college, but because we shared a love for the game, he had given it to me. And naturally, I put it next to my bed where I could turn and say good night to Michael right before I fell asleep. I remembered those nights when I would talk to him, asking him to please give me back my dad. Saying I would become the best basketball player ever so he would want to come and watch my games, and be proud that his daughter was actually making a name for herself in a sport that girls weren't encouraged to play. How else was I going to make sure I got his attention?

Mom told me she had no idea how to reach him. That he didn't want to be reached. So I decided, while pouring my hopes and dreams out to a yelling, slam-dunking Michael Jordan, that I was going to be so good, the newspapers and blogs would have to take notice of me. And my dad, in turn, would have to take notice of me too. Then maybe he would consider coming back. And I wouldn't have to wear these old, tattered, gray socks anymore just to pretend he was close to me.

My head snapped up when I heard my phone beep. Pulling it out of my backpack, I scanned my mom's text: *Please join us for dinner, Geri. Matt wants to treat us to steak.*

Telling on me, was he? And even worse, after eating a ham and cheese sandwich, he still had room for steak? No wonder Mom had to work for that promotion. She was feeding a garbage disposal. I flopped onto my tummy and my thumb flew across the screen: *I have homework, Mom.*

*Come on, Geri. Please. I'm really tired. I want to have a nice night out. With both of you.*

I hated it when she played the tired card. It always got to me. Maybe it was because I remembered what it was like back then, when we had all of a sudden found ourselves alone. How the light in her dark brown eyes had fizzled out and she had thrown herself into her work just so she could pay for me to go to school. We were lucky we had the house and Mom made enough to cover expenses, but we couldn't take trips anymore. Especially after she had to pay off her credit card bill on all the furniture she'd splurged on. I couldn't have the huge parties I grew up expecting, alongside a trip to Hong Kong or Singapore.

In the beginning, I was angry. I wanted my daddy. I wanted my life to go back to normal. I wanted my mom to be happy again, to be home with me and not at the office late into the evenings while Yaya Agnes and I watched Nickelodeon or did homework. But when I saw her crying in her bedroom one night, sobs that shook her body but didn't make a sound, I knew I had to stop being a brat. I had to cooperate and pull my weight. And I did.

I didn't ask for anything we couldn't afford, I tried really hard to do well in school, and I never complained. Until Matt showed up in the house one afternoon claiming to be some guy Mom met through a project at work. But I saw the way he smiled at her and the way she tried to keep from giggling whenever he cracked a lame joke. Two years later, he was on our couch, wanting to take us out to celebrate their anniversary. Excuse me while I begged Michael Jordan for the ability to keep my mouth shut and my thoughts from broadcasting themselves all over my face.

# Chapter 3

◻

"Ms. Lazaro!" My eyes flew open and I felt my neck snap as I tried to sit straight and pretend I was listening all along. Fat chance of that, but the least I could do was try.

"Yes, Ms. Mirasol, I'm listening. I'm listening." I could hear giggles ripple through the class. The girls were used to this. Heck, I was used to it.

"How could you be listening with your cheek plastered on your desk and drool trickling out of your mouth?"

At that, I rubbed my mouth against the sleeve of my white uniform. Really. Why she taught algebra was a complete mystery. With the way she spouted descriptions of my actions, or non-actions for that matter, she should have just been a creative writing teacher. And I definitely wouldn't be in *that* class.

She walked toward me and rapped her bony knuckles on the wooden desk where I was resting my elbows. I watched the beady eyes behind her purple wire-framed glasses narrow as she said, "Then solve the equation on the board. If you were indeed listening."

My eyes darted to the whiteboard, the mess of numbers and letters swimming before me. I didn't even know what equation she was talking about. How on earth was I going to solve it? I took a deep breath, about to apologize and lay out the story of my sad, pathetic life. About how my mom's boyfriend demanded we join him for dinner at a fancy restaurant and how they refused to go home until we sampled several plates of dessert despite my protests of being sleepy, tired, and in desperate need of reviewing for this grade 10 algebra class and—

"Ms. Lazaro, you're holding up the lesson." She leaned forward and I caught a whiff of strawberries. "I want to talk to you after class."

I looked down at my hands lying flat on my notebook. "Yes, miss."

When Ms. Mirasol turned back to the whiteboard, I felt something sharp poke my waist. I knew what it was. Without turning my head, I inched my left hand across my belly and took the folded note. I put it in between the pages of my algebra notebook and spread it out, making sure to cover most of it with my canvas pencil case.

*You ok?*

I checked to see if Ms. Mirasol was busy writing another jumble of numbers and letters on the board, then turned to face Simone, who had written me the note. She really could have just waited a few minutes to ask me, but this girl had no patience whatsoever. "I'm fine," I mouthed.

Her forehead creased and her lower lip jutted out. She shook her head then turned back to face the front of the classroom. I leaned back and let Ms. Mirasol's words drone over me as I waited for class to end. I felt my stomach twist into tiny Girl-Scout knots as I dreaded what Ms. Mirasol was going to say. No matter how many times you're pulled aside by the teacher, it doesn't get any less nerve-wracking. When the musical notes of the lunch bell jangled through the air, I let my classmates walk out the doors to head for the cafeteria before I approached the teacher's boxy, wooden desk.

I nodded at Simone to go ahead without me. She gave me that same sad look again. I rolled my eyes at her and said, "I'll be fine. Just go. Tell you about it later."

Taking a deep breath that hardly did anything to unfurl the knots in my tummy, I placed one foot in front of the other and trudged up to Ms. Mirasol. She was searching for something in her large tote bag. When she pulled it out, I felt one of those knots rise to my throat. I recognized it all right. It was her grading book.

"Geri." Her sharp voice was strangely soft and low. And she never called me Geri. This had to be bad. She looked at me through her purple glasses for a few seconds then flipped the grading book open. "I'm concerned about your grades. If you don't get at least an 85 on the mid-quarter test I'm giving next week, the record shows you're going to fail the quarter. And if that happens…"

"I'm off the basketball team." I knew this all too well.

"Not only that, dear." She pushed her glasses up her nose. "I will have to recommend, strongly recommend that you stop all other extra-curricular activities outside school as well."

My mouth dropped open but no sound came out. No, not ballet. She couldn't take away ballet. Or basketball.

"I know basketball isn't the only thing you do after class, right, Geri? How can you focus on school if you don't have time for anything else?"

"But—"

"This is for your own good. You have to focus on school. How do you expect to get into a good university with grades like this? Do you really think you can do it on a basketball scholarship? You're not academically challenged. I know that. You're just not focused. You can still get into a good school on your own merit."

"I don't care about getting into a good school!" My hands were balled up in fists by my sides.

"You do not mean that, Geri."

"Yes I do! What good is algebra to a professional ballet dancer? But I can't be a ballet dancer if you won't let me dance! And I already started late enough as it is. And I also need to play basketball because how else will my d—"

"She's right, Ms. Mirasol. Please give her a chance." I felt my eyes widen when I spotted Simone poke her head through the open doorway. Had she been listening all this time?

"Simone, this is a private conversation." Ms. Mirasol straightened up, her lips pursed.

"I'm sorry, I couldn't help it. I'm worried about Geri." She ducked her head back out of the doorway, but I had a funny feeling she was still hanging around listening to us. But that didn't matter. I turned back to Ms. Mirasol, the tears gathering in my eyes. I bit my lip praying they would somehow evaporate or seep back into my tear ducts.

"Ms. Mirasol, please."

"Geri, this is exactly what I'm worried about. You're throwing your future away by thinking like this. You need to exercise your brain as well, not just your limbs."

"But ballet and basketball require so much concentration! It's not just jumping around and—"

"You aren't listening to me." She put her hand on my shoulder. I flinched. I couldn't help it. But she didn't seem insulted. "This is for your own good, Geri. No extra-curricular activities if you get less than an 85 on the test. I will call your mom and let her know."

I swallowed the lump in my throat and looked up at the ceiling. "But right now..."

"Right now, I suggest you choose one. Basketball or ballet. And study for my test."

"But I swear, Ms. Mirasol, last night I had to be out with my mom and her boyfriend! It wasn't because of any of my activities!" It was a desperate plea and I could tell by the way her heavily penciled-in eyebrow shot up that she knew it. I already had a bad reputation in her class.

"Ms. Lazaro."

I heaved a sigh. She wasn't calling me Geri anymore. Gone was the caring teacher I could possibly win over. "Yes, Ms. Mirasol. I'll..." I bit back the words. I almost told her I was going to pass. But I knew I had no shot in hell. "I'll do my best."

"Your best might not be good enough, Ms. Lazaro."

"Of course it will be!"

I closed my eyes when I heard Simone's indignant squeak. She was going to get us both suspended if she kept this up.

I forced a smile at my algebra teacher. "Thank you, miss. I'll go reprimand Simone now." Before she could say anything more, I spun around, the long cotton fabric of my skirt swishing around my calves. I sped out of the classroom and saw my friend with her back pressed against the wall, her head turned to the side so she could eavesdrop like the spy she most likely imagined herself to be. "What are you doing here?"

She grabbed my hand and we both sprinted toward the cafeteria. "I didn't want you to say anything stupid. But you still did!" she muttered.

I shook my head and yanked her along. We had already lost precious break time talking to Ms. Mirasol. Plus, I was sure the lunch line was going to be twice as long now. When we pushed open the swinging double doors, we were greeted by the strong smells of fried fat and soy sauce. I wrinkled my nose. The whirring fans on the ceiling and the occasional spritz of cologne did little to dispel the aroma of grease that was probably embedded in the cement walls of our all-girls school. I spotted an empty table next to one of the stone pillars that held up the cafeteria's second floor. I motioned for Simone to line up while I kept other people from taking our table.

It didn't take her long to drop her tray of dumplings and iced tea next to me on the sticky tabletop. "Geri, whatever am I going to do with you? I swear, you are going to fail algebra."

I reached for one of her dumplings and popped it into my mouth. Her eyebrows dropped as I grinned and took another one with my fingers.

"I just have to figure out which after-school activity I need to give up." I finished off the dumpling I was holding and looked up to see if the lunch line was still long. I licked my fingers clean and wiped them on my skirt.

Simone tapped her hand on the table, bringing my attention back to her. "That means ballet, right?"

I blinked at her, knowing I shouldn't have said it that way. Simone was on the basketball team with me and she wasn't exactly happy about my ballet lessons taking time away from practice. She couldn't understand what she called my "new obsession." When I didn't answer her, she shook her head, the straight black hair cut close to her head hardly making a movement. "Don't tell me you're thinking of giving up basketball. I know it isn't game season but Coach wants us to practice for next season. And there are games—"

I didn't want to hear any more so I cut her off. "I haven't thought about it yet, Sim. Besides, as long as I don't have to keep going out with my mom and Matt, I'll be fine. It's their fault I didn't get to study last night."

A dreamy smile stole over the earlier anxiety on her face. "I haven't seen Matt in a while." She sighed. "Maybe we can study for the mid-quarter test in your house! Will he be there?"

Despite myself, I felt bubbles of amusement tickle my lips at the abrupt change. "You should talk to Helena and form a Matt Adoration Society." All of a sudden, a loud rumble erupted from the general vicinity of my stomach. I realized I had to go get food or run the risk of starving for the rest of the afternoon. I jumped up and headed for the end of the lunch line. I was surprised to find Simone right behind me, the dreamy look replaced by what resembled panic. "I'm serious, Geri. You can't bail on us."

Annoyance crept up my neck with hot, sticky feet. I narrowed my eyes at her. "Why do you think I'm going to bail on you? You know how I feel about the team. You know how I feel about the championship next year."

"I know how you feel about ballet." She folded her arms across her chest, the panic on her face giving way to something that looked like anger. Stubborn anger.

I chewed on my lip and studied her expression. I wasn't in the mood to get into a fight, though. Even if Simone clearly was. I looked up at the ceiling fans and let out a breath. "You know, Sim, I've never let you or the team down, right?"

"There's always a first time." She turned on her leather heel and I watched her march back to our table.

Blinking back the rage that was coloring my vision, I yelled, "Oh yeah?" I didn't care that the chatter of high-pitched voices came to a sudden stop. "Well, you can go suck eggs!"

Before Simone could come running back to punch me in the face, I felt a warm hand encircle my upper arm and pull me out of the cafeteria. Most likely to the principal's office. This day was getting better by the minute.

# Chapter 4

◁

"What were you thinking?" I turned to blink at Ms. Mirasol who was dragging me out the swinging doors and into the thick afternoon heat. I felt little pinpricks pierce my skin as the sun hit it. "Geri, you are already in big trouble as it is. Are you begging for a suspension?"

I winced, shielding my eyes from the sun's glare as we walked away from the scene of the crime. "I'm so sorry, Ms. Mirasol. At least that's all I told her to do."

I wasn't sure if the corners of her mouth twitched for a millisecond or if the haze from the sun was playing tricks on me. "It's a good thing no one from Student Services saw you. Well, the cafeteria ladies did but I don't think they're going to report you."

I gave Ms. Mirasol a small smile, hoping that meant she was going to let me go, and allow me to attempt to get that 85 on her exam. Because if I were suspended, even an 85 wouldn't save me. With my sorry academic record, the school higher ups might just decide to let me go for good.

"So are you going to go back in there and clean up this mess you started?"

I blinked. Did this mean...

"Am I free to go?" I held my breath while she released hers in a loud sigh.

"Yes, Geri. I can't believe you tried to sabotage your academic future so quickly after I tried to save it! But I still believe you can turn this around." She pushed her purple frames up her nose and stared me down.

I couldn't believe my ears. I jumped up and threw my arms around her. "Thank you so much, Ms. Mirasol! I promise to apologize to Simone and never scream at her again. In school anyway."

She took a step back and disentangled my arms from around her neck. "A thank you would have sufficed." But I noticed the twitch around her lips was back and definitely not due to the sun's glare this time.

"Thank you, miss." I tried to project as much dignity as I could in those three syllables.

She nodded her head. "But just in case anybody asks, I will be giving you extra work, ungraded work, in algebra. You need to submit it or I report what happened to your class adviser. Is that clear?"

"Yes, miss."

"Okay, let's go back inside. You and I need to eat. And you have amends to make."

I twisted my lips, not really looking forward to facing Simone again. But I knew where her anger was coming from, and I really couldn't blame her. She already felt I had abandoned her for ballet and now here I was clearly choosing to drop basketball—to drop her. And she had to know that wasn't what was happening here.

I followed Ms. Mirasol back through the double doors, letting them swing shut behind me. I made a beeline for Simone who was gesturing all over the place with her long arms, most likely complaining about me to the girls next to her. I felt rather than heard the students around our table quiet down. Of course they wanted to hear what I had to say after yelling at Simone and being dragged out by Ms. Mirasol mere moments ago. But I didn't want to give them a show. Let them create their own spectacle.

I pulled out the blue plastic chair next to Simone's untouched food tray and leaned forward, my forearms resting on the sticky table. I waited for her to acknowledge me. I wasn't going to beg for her attention. I was already about to apologize, right?

When she wouldn't turn to me, I swallowed my pride along with my saliva. "Sim, let's forget what happened, okay?"

I studied her face, waiting for her stony expression to soften. It took all of ten seconds. She swiveled her neck and her eyes locked with mine. I could see the struggle in them before she grimaced. "Yeah." Then she nodded toward the lunch line. "You better hurry. The line's shorter now, but there might not be anything good anymore. We might end up having to share these moisture-deprived dumplings."

I jumped up, gave Simone a big, relieved smile, and dashed to see what pathetic options I had left to fuel me for the rest of this frustrating day.

〰〰〰

The sky was turning a dark gray and the only light I had to see my way around the village park's basketball court came from the vanishing sun. I turned toward the basket, my left hand keeping the ball steady while my right took aim. I flicked my wrist and narrowed my eyes as the dark orange ball hurtled through the air. It bounced off the ring and fell to the right. I sprang forward to catch it when I saw two large hands close around the ball. I whipped my head up to glare at the intruder. No one had the gall to muscle in on me when I shot hoops.

Well, maybe just Simone, but she didn't have hands that almost covered half a basketball. My eyes widened when I saw who it was.

Although he wasn't in his white kimono—he was dressed in shorts and a regular tee—I recognized him. Dojo guy. With his hair cropped close to his head, an annoying smirk on his face, and my basketball in his beefy hands.

"That's mine."

"So come and get it." His upper body was bent, dribbling the ball in between his legs as he eyed me.

The muscles in my body tensed, ready to dive for the ball the split second he made a move. He lunged for my right but his gaze darted to my left, over my shoulder—where the basket was. As he spun to hurl the ball behind me, I jumped up and closed my arms around it. My heart thumped double time as I landed on my feet. I pivoted on the ball of my foot and bent my knees, my eyes on the hoop as I flung the basketball. It was only when I heard it swish as it fell through the net that I allowed myself to breathe again. Swallowing the triumphant yell that threatened to burst from my lips, I turned to face him. He was staring at me with a strange look on his face. I wanted to say it was a look of awe and admiration, but I knew better.

"First to shoot ten. That was my first shot."

A smile crossed his features as he wiped his hands on his shorts. "You're on."

The next few minutes were probably the most intense I had spent outside playing an actual game. Dojo guy was pretty good. In fact, the fight was so close, my shirt clung to my body and I found myself dragging my arm across my eyes every few minutes to dry my sweat. I had never tried this hard during training. Coach would be proud. Hell, Simone would be impressed. After ducking and leaping out of Dojo guy's reach, I raised my arms over my head after I shot my last basket, allowing that scream of victory to finally escape my lungs.

"That's what you get for thinking you can take me on." The adrenaline pumped through my veins, making me feel like I was on top of the world. And all I had really done was score two baskets more than he did. But the victory felt stronger than when we won the game that entered us into the semi-finals last year.

He was grinning up at me, sprawled on the ground, his hand tight around a water bottle. "You're good."

I tried to swallow the smug smile that was stealing over my warm face. "Surprised?"

"I had no idea what to think." He tossed his water bottle at me and I closed a hand around it. "But I have to admit, this makes more sense than the ballet."

After tilting the bottle all the way up to drain the last few drops, I swallowed and frowned at him. "Because I don't look girly, right? You've said as much."

"I didn't mean that in a bad way." He scrambled to his feet, blocking out the sun. Fine, it had already set and the park street lamps were flickering on one by one. I just wanted to make fun of how tall he was. Not that it was a bad thing. But I was scrambling for more bad things to associate with him.

"Of course you didn't." I rolled my eyes. I jogged away from him to retrieve my ball when I heard the rumble of a car engine. I looked up to see Matt's silver sedan pull up next to the courts. I wrinkled my brow. What was he doing here? I specifically told Mom I could walk home. Besides, it was a Friday. No school the next day. Oh crap, did this mean he wanted to have dinner out again and that he was here to take me home to change?

I contemplated my chances of making a run for it when I heard the car door slam. Too late. "Hey, Bas! You ready for me to whip your ass?"

My mouth fell open. What was going on? They knew each other?

Matt was in a loose gray tee and black jogging pants. I'd never seen him look so dressed down before. He was always ready to impress when he was in Mom's company.

"What are you doing here?" I blurted out as the guys high-fived each other. So much for my sneaky escape.

"Geri!" Matt smiled and held up his hands as if I had a gun pointed at his chest, which sometimes, I wished I did just to scare him away. I had no evil, violent tendencies, at least none that involved blowing anyone's brains out. Not yet anyway. "I swear, I didn't know you were here. I'm not stalking you."

I knew he expected me to laugh or acknowledge his joke but I just walked past him to pick up my bag. I didn't want to hang around him and Dojo guy. That would just be double the annoyance.

"Are you always this rude?"

I swung around, my eyes narrowed into slits. How dare Dojo guy say that to me! I marched up to him and poked his chest with my finger, a small part of my brain registering that my finger made contact with solid flesh. "You have no right to ask me that. You don't even know me."

I noticed his eyebrows meet as he looked down at me. But before anything could come out of his mouth, I felt a hand close around my shoulder. "It's okay, Geri. You've probably had a rough day."

"Why are you making excuses for me, Matt?" Yeah, I know. If I were Dojo guy and had no idea what the family dynamic was in this situation, I'd think I was a brat of the highest caliber.

But really, why was he so freaking nice? Couldn't he be normal for once? "You don't always have to be so nice to me!" Without bothering to ask how they knew each other, I stormed off, the earlier high from my victory a distant and now infuriating memory.

# Chapter 5

I loved Saturday mornings. If we didn't have a game, I was free to spend them dancing with Helena. After our eight a.m. class, Teacher Justine requested our assistance with her baby ballet students. They were so cute in their miniature pink skirts and soft ballet shoes, jumping around trying their best to keep their arms and legs straight. I'd sometimes wonder what my life would be like if I had started ballet as early as five or even four years old. Maybe I'd have a stronger arabesque or a tighter pirouette and wouldn't be running to Helena every few minutes to ask for tips.

In between classes, Helena and I would run through different routines. I found them helpful especially now that our recital was nearing. But today was different. I woke up with a headache because I had spent the entire night talking to my Michael Jordan poster. I told him I needed to make a decision or else I was going to fail tenth grade. It hurt me that I had to give up something I loved, and maybe that even meant giving up the dream of my dad showing up in my life again because I was such an awesome ball player. But I couldn't exactly fail high school, could I? And—I turned away when I said this— it pained me to admit to Michael that I loved ballet more. I was afraid he'd tilt his slam-dunking head down an inch so his eyes would no longer be focused on the basketball—but on me. He'd close his mouth and glower at me for abandoning the game we both adored. I fell asleep with my face turned away from the poster. But I still imagined Michael's eyes boring into my back, disappointed and angry.

Back at the studio, Helena pressed down on my shoulders. "Geri, feel how tight they are? You need to relax them even more. This dance requires a softer silhouette." I sighed and dropped the arms I held above my head, abandoning my pose.

While we were waiting for the next class, Teacher Justine slipped out for a bit to make some calls. So Helena and I decided to work on a new dance.

"Maybe I need a quick break." I didn't want to tell her what the real problem was. I could already imagine the sympathy in her eyes. And I didn't want that. But at least, I didn't have to worry about her being disappointed that I was choosing ballet over basketball. And we definitely weren't going to get into a fight the way Simone and I had in the cafeteria.

Helena shook her dainty head, her hair not in a perfect bun the way it usually was, but in a high ponytail with glittery star-shaped clips on both sides. It made her look softer, sweeter, if that was even possible. "You don't need a break. You need to dance. But a dance you're already an expert at." She drifted toward Teacher Justine's speakers, her fingers flitting across the phone plugged into them. The music that filled the studio, empty except for the two of us, was as familiar to me as the sound of a basketball thumping across a wooden court. I grinned at her and leapt to the center of the studio, facing the large floor-to-ceiling mirrors. I extended my arms in a circle above my head and let the music drench my senses. I closed my eyes and allowed my body to follow the rhythm I had learned a few months ago. Combinations, twirls, and extensions I knew so well, I didn't even have to think of what came next.

This. This was why I was willing to give up basketball. This was why I turned my back on Michael Jordan's accusing glare so I could get some sleep. This was what made life worth living. As I soared, landed on my feet, rose on my toes, my arms weaving in and out, up and down, my legs bending, stretching, extending behind me, before me, above my head, I felt the weariness lift off me like water droplets evaporating in the warmth of the midday sun. The way that great ball of flame bestowed life was the same way dance revitalized me. I ended with my head inclined upward, my right arm above it as if reaching for the sky, my left arm and leg stretched to the side.

I was released from my trance by hands clapping and light feet bouncing around. I let go of my pose and turned to see Helena bobbing up and down, her filmy skirts fluttering around her thighs. "You were wonderful, Geri!" She glided toward me and threw her arms around my neck. I hugged her back, filled with gratitude that she had set me back on course. And not just so I could learn the next dance, but so I could take comfort in the fact that I had made the right decision.

"No one can do that dance justice like you." Helena's smile was beatific. I knew she could do it better, but it didn't matter. Because I knew how I felt while dancing it, and that was what mattered to me. "And I think someone agrees with me," she added, a teasing lilt in her tone. I followed her eyes as she glanced out the glass window near the entrance.

I blinked when I saw a tall, solid figure in that same white martial arts uniform I'd first glimpsed him in. The same guy I had just defeated in a game of one-on-one the night before. His mouth was hanging open but when his eyes met mine, he shut it and returned a smirk to his face. Maybe he thought that could pass for a smile. Someone needed to tell him that it didn't. I didn't bother to acknowledge him and turned back to Helena. She widened her eyes at me and whispered, "Aren't you going to say hi?"

"No. Why should I?"

She tilted her head to the side and tugged at my skirts. "Because you want to introduce him to me."

Defying the great urge to roll my eyes, I swiveled back to the window and motioned with my hand for him to come in. He raised an eyebrow and pointed at himself. I knew he was mocking me. I looked at Helena again, whose porcelain skin was turning a pretty shade of pink. I grabbed her hand and marched to the door. I pulled it open. "Come in already."

He grinned and stepped into the brightly lit studio, the scenario quite the opposite of our first meeting. "Hi, I'm Bas Mercado." I felt like I was watching a cheesy film with bad actors as Dojo guy bent his massive shoulders and held out his hand to Helena. She in turn, took his paw—yes, that's what it was—and curtseyed. Was this really happening? We were teenagers for crying out loud. And this was not the Regency period. What were these two doing? Must have been the outfits. But then again, I was in my tights, leo, and skirt, but I wasn't curtseying to anyone.

"Wasn't Geri awesome?"

Wait, what? Why was Helena talking about me?

He lifted his shoulders in a shrug. "I wouldn't know. I don't exactly watch ballet."

Helena lifted her hand to hide the giggles escaping her lips. "That's not what your expression told me. I saw your face while she danced."

If I didn't love her so much, I would have hooked my foot around her leg to send her crashing to the floor. What did she think she was doing? What was even more baffling was Dojo guy's face. I wasn't sure if he really was turning red or if that was how his face normally looked. The only thing I studied last night while setting my sights on defeating him were his eyes. And how they had a slight downward tilt at the ends, especially when he smiled.

"I was shocked, that's all." Dojo guy grinned at me.

I put my hands on my hips, on the waistband of my skirt. "Fine. Say it."

"Say what?" He took a step back. I glanced down and noticed I had put one foot forward.

"That you didn't think I could dance ballet."

I heard Helena muttering something about the basketball uniform not being the cause of my combative nature after all.

"Well, after you wiped the floor with me yesterday in basketball, I didn't think you could dance too. I swear, that's all, Geri."

Helena smiled. "And when you aren't dancing, Geri, you don't exactly move like a ballerina. Not that it's a bad thing."

I sighed. I knew this. And it normally didn't bother me. I didn't know why it annoyed me so much when Dojo guy brought it up.

"So you two played basketball yesterday?" Helena tilted her head to the side, the end of her ponytail brushing across her shoulder.

"Yeah, I didn't know what I was getting into!" Dojo guy laughed, his eyes doing that downward dipping thing again. Well, at least he wasn't a sore loser. He wasn't bringing up how I lost it after Matt showed up either. So he got points for that. Maybe enough for me to let my guard down. Just a little bit.

"Geri's awesome. But whenever we watch her games, I never know what's going on!" Helena's laugh tinkled like wind chimes dancing in a soft breeze.

"You play *and* you dance? When do you sleep?" Dojo guy gaped at me. Well, I would have been proud of myself if I weren't forced to give one up for the sake of my academic survival.

I was saved from answering when Teacher Justine walked through the door. She walked up to us and peered into Dojo guy's face.

"Good morning, young man. Are you here to join our class?"

I frowned at her but noticed her lips twitching. Oh great, don't tell me my ballet teacher was flirting with this guy too!

"Good morning, ma'am. I'm Bas Mercado." Dojo guy smiled. "I wish I could join you—especially after watching the way Geri moves—but I have an aikido class in a few minutes." He bowed again at Teacher Justine and held out his hand. I watched my teacher's dainty one disappear in his and wondered what it would feel like to have that happen to mine too. I shook my head to expel the thought and crossed my arms over my chest to block out any more weirdness. Besides, I was pretty sure he was mocking me again with that line about how I move.

When Dojo guy finally left the studio and Teacher Justine stepped away to prepare for the next class, Helena began hopping up and down, squealing. I raised both hands and tried to shush her. She was behaving worse than the little kids who were walking in, their eyes widening at the spectacle my friend was causing. "You didn't tell me you were friends!" Helena whacked me on the arm. Okay, fine, she tapped my bicep. I don't think whack and Helena should co-exist in one sentence. Unless it was me doing the whacking, of course. Which was something I was so tempted to do at that moment.

I covered my arm with my hand and frowned at her. "We're not friends!"

"But you played basketball yesterday." She lifted a slender finger and, in one fluid movement, wagged it at me.

I raised my eyes to the ceiling, trying to keep my voice down. "It wasn't like I invited him to join me. I was in the park shooting hoops, trying to get my mind off school, and he just grabbed the ball."

"What was he doing there?" she whispered. There was an urgency in her voice because Teacher Justine was already herding the little girls in a straight line and we were expected to help out.

I began walking toward the girls, Helena gliding next to me. "He was there to meet Matt."

"Matt!"

I knew it. Every time I mentioned him, Helena got all swoony.

"Yeah. Yuck."

"Stop that, Geri. You're being mean. He's nothing but nice to you."

"You just know that from what I tell you. You don't know that for sure." I turned to Helena and stuck my tongue out at her.

"Teacher, Ate Geri just stuck her tongue out!" Oh crap.

"I'm sorry, Teacher Justine. I'm sorry, girls. I won't do it again." I covered my mouth with both hands. The little ones began to titter. I snuck a glance at Teacher Justine and she just shook her head at me but didn't say anything else.

Helena and I took our places behind the girls and kept our mouths closed throughout the lesson. While helping the little ballerinas straighten their legs, point their toes, and tuck in their tummies, my thoughts kept straying to my situation. Sure, I could give up basketball, have Simone mad at me for a few months tops, but I still had the problem of finding a way to score an 85 on that test. Giving up basketball didn't mean I was automatically going to make the grade. How was I going to catch up by myself? I needed help but I wasn't going to get it from my friends. They were getting by but they weren't math geniuses either. I needed another plan. But what? I didn't think Mom could afford to hire me a tutor.

After class, as Helena and I sat on the soft, wooden floor putting on our shoes and getting our things together, she slid closer to me. "I think you should be nicer to him, Ger."

"Who? Matt?" Since *everyone* was telling me to be nicer to Matt.

"Well, yes, Matt." Her cheeks dimpled. "But I was talking about Bas. He watched you dance. You know what that means." Her smile was sure, confident. Like she knew all the answers to that math test I had to ace. Problem was, I didn't. I scrutinized her face, trying to remember if we talked about this before, but nothing was coming to me.

"Wait a minute." I put a hand on her arm. "I have no idea what that means. All I know is that I was dancing and he was outside watching. Period. Why are you smiling at me like that?"

Helena's eyes rolled to the back of her head. "Any guy who watches you dance will fall in love with you, Geri."

She said it so matter-of-factly that I sat there stunned.

"Geri, you dance like a dream."

"No, that's you, Helena."

She bent her head as if to acknowledge something she had known all along. "Yes but there's something different about the way you move. Trust me on this."

We pulled ourselves off the floor and walked out the door. My mind was spinning with what Helena just told me. I mean, yes, I loved ballet and I knew I was good at it but I never heard Helena or anyone else describe my dancing that way. Never mind that Dojo guy did have his mouth open when I turned to look at him. He was probably just surprised. I felt my lips turn up and no matter how hard I bit down on them, they wouldn't straighten.

As I stepped out into the parking lot, the midday sun beating down on my shoulders, I spotted someone standing by the curb, his eyes on his cellphone. Surprise, surprise, it was Dojo guy. Of course his class just had to end the same time ours did. Helena skipped over to him before I could grab her shoulder and yank her back.

"Hi, Bas! What are you doing here?" Her dimples peeked out as she smiled up at him.

"I had to reply to this text. I'm on my way to my car now." He grinned back at her. I crossed my arms over my chest, watching to see what was going down.

"Oh, here's my car now." Her fingers flew to her pursed lips. "Geri's ride isn't here yet, though."

I closed my eyes for a few seconds, praying for strength, patience, and the self-control I needed to keep me from bopping her on the head. I knew exactly what she was trying to do.

"I can wait with her." He turned his head to glance at me. "That is, if she doesn't mind." Then the smirk emerged.

Helena put an arm around me and pulled me close. Then in my ear, she whispered, "Be nice."

"Ugh," I mumbled back.

I plastered a smile on my face and watched her slide into her sleek, black car. Of all days for Mom to agree to pick me up. I should have just texted her and told her I was going to catch a ride with Helena. Now I had to talk to Dojo guy while I waited for God knew how long.

"You don't have to wait with me, you know." I shuffled over to the tired looking wooden bench that rested next to the building entrance.

It took him all of three strides to plop down next to me, a half-smile on his face. "Nah, I've got nothing better to do. Besides, I have a proposal for you."

I glanced at him over my shoulder. "Feeling close, aren't we?"

"Hear me out, Geri." I didn't notice that dimple on his right cheek before. He and Helena had a matching set.

"Fine. Shoot."

# Chapter 6

◻

Bas quirked an eyebrow as he contemplated my face, as if assessing whether or not I meant what I had just said. After a few seconds of silence, I turned away and dragged the back of my hand across my forehead to wipe away the beads of sweat that the midday Manila sun squeezed from my skin.

"You don't have to tell me about it if you're worried I won't believe you." Don't ask me where that came from. Maybe I just got belligerent whenever he was around. Maybe it was my primal response to his martial arts outfit.

His rich laugh boomed outward, engulfing my entire body in its grasp. "Okay, here goes. What do you think of dancing with me?"

When I snapped my neck to face him, the small muscles strained in protest. "You're kidding, right?"

His eyes, dipping down at the ends, were a dark brown that reminded me of my dad's worn-out leather dress shoes. A slight twinge pricked my chest.

"I'm not. Our aikido school is going to have a demonstration in a couple of weeks and Sensei wanted to do something different. At first, I thought he wasn't thinking straight. Why do something different when what you're selling is the martial art itself? But when I saw you dance..."

"You wanted to do ballet too? Okay, I get that." I smirked.

"No! Not that there's anything wrong with that!" He fumbled, his eyes no longer focused on me. They darted to his large hands resting on his lap, the car zooming down the street, and finally, back to me. "I mean—" Little round beads dotted his forehead. He reached into the pocket of his loose, dirty white pants and pulled out a white handkerchief. Dabbing it over his face, he shook his head. "This is coming out all wrong."

Something snapped inside me, and like warm molten lava cake freshly sliced open with a dessert fork, I felt something hot and gooey ooze out and coat my insides. "I'm sorry, Bas. I'm just giving you a hard time. What did you have in mind?"

His deep, dark eyes widened in disbelief and I bit the inside of my lower lip to keep from laughing.

"I saw this exhibition on YouTube where performers combined ballet with karate. With how fluid the movements are in aikido, it just hit me as I was watching you that we could do something like that."

I frowned, and a look of frustration crossed his features. It wasn't that I didn't think it was cool. The idea itself was some kind of awesome. What I wasn't too hot about was dancing with *him*. Before I could tell him this, he jumped up and stood right in front of me, blocking my view of the street. I leaned back, wondering what he was about to do when he raised his beefy arms above his head and attempted to form a circle with them. The grin on his face was goofy. I crossed my arms over my chest and tightened my lips into a straight line.

"How did it go? Was it something like this?" he asked.

My mouth fell open when I realized he was going through the movements of the solo I had danced in the studio earlier that morning. He stretched his arms to his sides, his right extended over his head, then lifted his leg and tried to raise it higher than waist level. His sturdy hands were spread wide, as if waiting to catch or stop something floating in the air. His eyebrows rested low on his forehead in concentration, his eyes narrowed as if trying to remember what he had seen. After attempting a pirouette, which he tried to do on one foot, I snapped my mouth shut, straightened my back, and pushed myself up with my feet. I planted myself next to him and, with hands on my hips, said, "*This* way."

I balanced myself by putting my arms in fourth position, one arm curled in a half-circle in front of me and the other lengthened to the side, yet still a soft curve. With my feet turned out at opposite ends with a little space in between, I lifted myself on my left foot and raised my right to slightly touch the side of my knee. I spun with my arms in a circle before me, holding my body as straight as I could. Then, with a smug smile, I lengthened my right leg and tucked it back in, again and again, turning several times, till I heard a gasp next to me.

"Now you're just showing off."

I landed in the position I started, my arms reaching for an unseen dance partner. I glanced at him over my shoulder and raised an eyebrow in challenge. "Care to top that?"

He hopped on one foot and started spinning in sporadic bursts of speed, wobbling to the left and then to the right, till he threw out a leg to keep from falling. He hopped closer and closer, his arms flailing, trying to straighten himself so he could continue the spin, but either the force of gravity was too strong or he slipped on a tiny, unseen pebble. My feet, no longer in any ballet position, felt like superglue had been spread on their soles. I threw out my arms, whether to catch him or to protect myself, I didn't know. But when his weight and heft came crashing into me, I felt his body twist, his arms coming around me, securing my back against his solid chest. I took a deep breath, about to elbow him away, when I felt him curl his shoulder inward as we both plummeted to the ground.

The world was upside down for a few seconds. My breath caught in my throat, and my heart started beating faster than it had the last time we played one-on-one. Being this close, I was afraid he'd stink like sweat and gym socks, but he didn't. I caught a whiff of shampoo and—was that the sharp tang of rubbing alcohol? In a few seconds, we were upright again, he was on his haunches in a crouch and I was in between his knees, locked there like a child he was protecting from a big, bad, birthday mascot.

I didn't know how long I stayed there, it must have been less than a nanosecond, but I felt like the entire roll had happened in excruciating slow motion. I gulped down the lump in my throat and scrambled to my feet.

"You...how did you—"

"I know. It was pretty pathetic." He straightened up and grinned at me.

"No, that roll or whatever you call it." I pointed at the ground, twirling my hand, trying to get my noisy thoughts under control.

"Yes. That was a roll."

"You kept me from getting hurt." I didn't know why I was so stunned. Didn't they fall and roll all the time while practicing aikido? I guess I never thought I'd be in the middle of one, like a piece of kani stuffed in a California Maki, only more snug and safe.

He shrugged but his grin softened. We stood there looking at each other for a few seconds till he coughed into his fist. "But see how we could do something like that?"

I tilted my head to the side, glad I was beginning to feel like my regular self again. "Well, maybe not exactly like that. You can leave the ballet to me."

"But don't you see, you can do some turns and jumps and I can do some falls, rolls, maybe a few sword exercises." His dark eyes were alight with the possibility of something neither of us had ever witnessed before. The fudge that had earlier covered my insides when I decided to stop being mean to him? It began to bubble as a fire lit up within me as well.

"It could be like an Asian fairytale!"

"Uh, I don't know about that." He stepped back and studied me from the corner of his eyes.

I raised my hands to the light blue sky, so light it was almost white, and let out a gust of air from somewhere deep inside. "I don't know how you expect us to work together when we can't agree on anything." I swiveled on my toes to peer up and down the street, willing my mom's small, dark green sedan to come rumbling by. When I still didn't spot it, I trudged back to the short, wooden bench by the wall and plopped down on it.

I didn't have to wait long before I felt the bench sag under me as Bas sat down as well. "We just have to try. Come on, Geri. For one brief shining moment, you thought it was an awesome idea too. Right?"

A laugh escaped me despite my irritation. "Yes, King Arthur."

He laughed too. That rich laughter again. "You got me. I didn't take you for a *Camelot* fan."

"My dad used to watch it a lot when I was a kid. We'd sing the songs together. He was Arthur and Mom was Guinevere. I was Lancelot because I loved his song about being perfect." I pressed my lips together. I hadn't thought about that in a while. A long while. The pain that King Arthur felt at the end of the musical when he was remembering how beautiful his life and his Camelot used to be before it was ruined, destroyed, was the same pain I felt whenever memories of my dad popped into my consciousness. I shook my head. "But yeah, I did. Thought your idea had potential, I mean."

"And that move I just did?" He lifted his hands and moved

them as if he were twining yarn around them. "You can do that in basketball. If you fall. All you need to do is learn how to roll properly and you can avoid injury."

"I won't be playing basketball anymore." What the hell? I wasn't supposed to say *that*. I was about to tell him that this idea of his did not involve me learning any aikido. It was about us doing our own art separately but alongside one another. But I sometimes had no control over what came out of my mouth.

"Why not?" He tapped me on the knee. "Is it because I was such a daunting opponent that you can't bear to face me ever again?"

I turned my entire body to face him, then backed my butt up a few inches seeing how close he was on that short bench. "In what alternate universe did you play basketball against me and win? From what I recall, on Planet Earth, I won that game."

He held up his paws, his eyes closing as guffaws convulsed through his body. "Man, you can't take a joke, can you?"

"Not when it comes to the truth being twisted, no."

"I think it's because you can't bear to lose."

"Well, that too."

"So if you can't stand being a loser, why quit basketball? You've definitely got game." His thick eyebrows melted together.

I dug into my ballet bag for my phone, hoping for an excuse not to answer him. I saw a message on my lock screen. Mom. She was on her way but would be later than usual because of something or other. I tossed it back inside and swallowed. "I'm failing algebra." I wrinkled my nose, keeping my gaze on the cracks in the gray asphalt. "My teacher said I need to give up one of my extracurriculars so I can do well on my next exam."

"And you chose to keep ballet." I listened for judgment in

his tone, condemning me for making the wrong decision, the way Michael Jordan probably did. But I found none.

"Yes."

"I can see why. If I hadn't seen you dance today, I would have said you're not thinking straight. But it would be a waste if you didn't dance, Geri."

It felt like there were invisible strings tied to the ends of my mouth and a puppet master was pulling them up. It's not like I wanted to smile at him, but my mouth apparently did. And that was how my mother found me. Found us.

She was already leaning out the car window, her arm sticking up, making wide arcs through the air. "Geri! Yoohoo!"

Grabbing my things, I jumped up and was about to bolt for the car when Bas put his hand on my arm. "Let me know what you decide, okay? The demonstration is in a few weeks. There's still time."

I nodded, not trusting myself to speak. Who knew what else would come out of my traitorous mouth? I dashed to the car and yanked the passenger door open without even saying hello to my mother whose eyes were burning holes into me.

When I pulled the dark gray seatbelt across me and clicked its lock into place, I felt my mom poke me in the tummy. "Ow!" I slapped her hand away even if it didn't hurt. I knew what she was up to and it wasn't what I was in the mood for. Ever.

"Who is he?"

How could she not even be stepping on the gas? Bas was still standing there, probably waiting for us to drive away, for goodness' sake.

"Just some guy I met in class."

My eyes widened in panic when she turned to him and gave him a wave. No. No. No. And yes, of course his face split into a grin as he waved back. *Please do not ask him to come over.* "Mom, can we please go already?"

She sighed and turned the key in the ignition. "Sometimes, Geri, you are so uptight."

"Always, Mom."

"He's so cute."

"Yeah, you'd think so."

"But how did you meet him in class?" Thank God her eyes were no longer on me as she concentrated on shifting into the main road. "He was in a gi."

"A what now?"

"A martial arts uniform."

"Oh that's what that kimono thing is."

"Yes. So is Teacher Justine teaching karate too?" She giggled. I looked up at the fuzzy ceiling of our car and begged God for patience.

"No, he's in an aikido class next to ours."

"Well, I think he's really cute. And it's not a subjective kind of cute. It's a cute that all girls and guys attracted to guys would agree on."

"What?" What was she smoking? Seriously.

"You know, like Matt. He's conventionally cute. This guy of yours is too."

"Ugh, Mom, can you just not?"

But instead of reprimanding me for being rude, she reached down and pushed the radio power button, allowing music to blast through the car. Her music. Music from the 1990s. Music I grew up with. As if that same puppet master were controlling my strings, I ended up screaming along with her and Alanis Morissette that it wasn't fair to deny us of the cross we had to bear because he, whoever he was, oughta know about the mess he left when he went away. Mom and I loved this song. And I was pretty sure we were both thinking of my dad as we sang it. But while we shouted the words together with Alanis, the hurt didn't seem so precious or so sacred, the way it usually did. It was out there and it was okay. And right now, even if Mom was being annoying about Bas, she and I were okay.

# Chapter 7

▽

I could smell the hotdogs sizzling on the slick, rolling grill. The meaty, juicy aroma made me feel as if a leak had sprouted in my mouth as I anticipated sinking my teeth into the red, oily, processed tube of meat. I felt rather than heard the banging of the drums as my heart matched its beat, together with the roar of the crowd as it chanted words I couldn't figure out. I tapped my foot, wondering if the girl manning the stall would give me a dark look if I asked when the hotdogs would be ready. I did just ask her a few seconds ago.

"Geri, why are you still here? The game is about to start!" Helena materialized by my side, tugging on my bare arm.

Earlier that morning, I was rolling around in bed wondering which algebra topic I was going to tackle for the day. I really should have started on it the afternoon before, but I just wanted to lie down and sleep. I rationalized that I had danced all morning and had even been nice to Bas, so that exempted me from doing any work I didn't enjoy. Besides, I had all day on Sunday anyway. But when Simone texted me saying there was a soccer game that afternoon between our school and its rival, well, I just had to go, right? I dragged Helena along since she studied in one of those expensive, international schools that never gave any homework.

"You know I need you to explain what happens." She frowned at me, her thinly arched eyebrows lowering.

I turned to look at hotdog girl and widened my eyes at her. She shrugged and said, "It's almost ready, ma'am."

I put a hand on my grumbling tummy. Lunch was hours ago, and I needed sustenance now. I turned to the field, a uniform sea of bright green, with the players in two separate huddles. "Ma'am?" I swung my head back to see the glistening hotdog nestled in between the folds of a soft, cream-colored bun. Finally.

"Thank you!" I tossed a fifty-peso bill on the counter, grabbed the hotdog, and we sprinted for our seats next to Simone. We were about to sit down when everyone around us jumped to their feet. The players let out a rallying cry and jogged to their places on the field. My eyes were glued to the players of our team.

I loved watching women's sports. There was something so empowering about seeing girls do what many people tell us we can't or shouldn't be doing. This coming from the girl who decided to pick ballet, right?

"Hey, what did I miss?" The deep, masculine voice yelled in my ear and I almost dropped my hotdog.

"Why are you here?" I yelled back. The noise around us was deafening as someone from the other team stole the ball from between the feet of one of our players. I was torn between screaming along with the crowd and asking Bas why I couldn't get rid of him. To think I only met him three days ago.

"Helena messaged me. Told me I might want to catch the game with you guys." He leaned his head back a little bit. "I thought you knew."

I looked at him like he just suggested I jump onto the field and grab the ball with my hands. "Doesn't matter. You can sit over there next to Helena."

"But there's space right here." My head bent as I followed his movement. Then I felt his hand close around mine, the one holding the hotdog. "I haven't had lunch. Can I take a bite?"

"What? No!" But my voice was drowned out when people leapt to their feet again as apparently, someone scored a goal. "See you made me miss that!" I glowered at him, taking a big bite out of my hotdog. I was so distracted, I didn't even take note of how it tasted. Turning to my right, I nudged Helena with my elbow. "What is he doing here?"

Her dimples winked at me as her eyes crinkled up. She leaned forward and gave Bas a little wave. "Hey, Bas! Glad you could make it!" She rose on her dainty toes and spoke in my ear. "I found him on Facebook and he posted something about not doing anything today so I told him about the game."

"Then let him sit beside you!" I didn't know why I had to be the one to take care of him when she brought this upon us—brought him upon me.

When the crowd quieted down after the opposing team had scored their goal, Simone planted herself in between me and Helena, forcing us to scoot over on the long, wooden bench. "Who is that, Geri?" She poked my arm.

"Hi, I'm Bas. Geri's friend." I twisted my head to see him leaning forward, smiling at Simone.

Simone flashed him a wide smile then pointed at herself. "Simone." She waved her hand in Helena's general direction, her eyes still on Bas. "This is Helena. I didn't know Geri invited another friend to the game."

"She didn't either." He laughed and, though I felt like a petulant child, I tossed what remained of the hotdog sandwich into my mouth, wiped my fingers on my denim shorts, and crossed my arms. I kept my eyes trained on the field. Let them talk over me if they wanted. I could ignore them. I was good at that. Got lots of practice whenever I was around Mom and Matt. "Do you dance too? I didn't see you in the studio."

Who was this friendly impostor? What did he do with Dojo guy who, only a few days ago, was all frowns, glowers, and snark? Oh wait, that sounded like me. But see, I was here, being my regular self. I wasn't pretending to be all friendly and charming.

Simone's hand flew to her chest. I was watching from the corner of my eye. "You dance ballet too? That is awesome. Male ballet dancers are so strong and jump so high! You'd be amazing on the basketball court."

Give me a break. Did he look like a dancer to her? And really, I creamed him in basketball. I could hear Helena explaining how we all met and Bas was joining in over my head. Why weren't they paying attention to the game? We were down by one, for crying out loud.

"Right, Geri?"

Huh? I inclined my head toward him. "I wasn't listening. I was paying attention to the game." I meant it to berate him, let him know why he was there in the first place. But by the look of his grin, he didn't seem to get it.

"I told them about our collaboration."

I stared at him, my mouth falling open. "I didn't even agree yet!"

"Oh, come on, Geri. You know you want to." His eyes. Dipping on the sides. Again.

"It sounds wonderful, Geri! You should do it!" Helena reached over Simone, her hand resting on my clenched fist. I didn't realize my hands were balled tight. I relaxed them.

"Yeah, well, as long as it's after the algebra test next week then maybe you can do it." Simone arched an eyebrow at me.

That stupid test. Stupid algebra.

"Yeah, all you have to do is ace it and you can go back to playing basketball, right?"

Did Bas just say that? I peered up at him, clocking his expression. There was no snark, no frown. His features were arranged in a way I had never seen before. Did that look like concern? Why did this guy think we were friends when we hardly knew each other?

"Maybe." I allowed a small smile to peek through my dark, gray cloud of a mood. When I turned back to see how our team was doing, I felt a strong buzzing against my thigh. I dug into the pocket of my shorts and saw Mom's name and face on the screen. She knew where I was. She said yes. Why was she calling me now?

I jumped down from where we sat and hurried away from the crowd so I could hear her. "Mom?"

"Geri, come home right now."

"Why, Mom? The game just started!"

"I just got a call from school. You shouldn't be at a game when you have an exam to study for."

Crap. There was a reason I didn't tell her about the test.

"I don't think I can ask Simone or Helena to take me home while they're watching the game." Pathetic excuse. Helena had a driver and Mom knew that.

"Geri." Her voice sounded almost like a growl, like she was making a supreme effort not to lose her temper with me.

"Okay."

I slid the phone back into my pocket and dragged my feet back to my friends. This was the worst feeling ever, having to leave in the middle of a game, when the adrenaline was high and the school spirit needed a boost you were certain only your presence could give. And what for? To go home to a mother who was going to ground you for the rest of your life. Or till you passed a certain exam. I could have disobeyed her and stayed till the end, but my mind flashed back to that time I saw Mom crying on her bed after Dad left. Something inside me twisted. Even with Matt hanging around making me miserable, it was really just the two of us left in this family. And I couldn't ruin that by straining our relationship even more.

Putting my hand on Helena's shoulder, I asked if her driver could take me home. Her forehead creased and she nodded her head, pulling out her phone to send him a text.

Bas leaned his elbows on his denim-clad knees, watching us. "What's going on?"

"My mom called. I have to go home." I tried to keep the emotion out of my voice.

He got to his feet and held out his hand to me. "I can take you."

"But Helena's driver can just—"

"Oh, he went on an errand for my mom." Helena dropped her phone back in her tote, blinking up at me.

I glared at her. Was this another one of her ploys?

She smiled back at me. "Sorry, Geri. But if Bas can take you home, that would be better, right?"

I rolled my eyes and bit back a groan. "Fine." I nudged Simone on the shoulder, told her what was going on, and followed Bas out the stadium.

"Thanks." My eyes were on my sneakers as we crossed a dirt path to get to his car. "For taking me home."

"Can't risk your mom tearing your hair out."

"My teacher called her. I can't believe she called her on a Sunday!"

"Hey, it's going to be okay."

"No, it's not. You don't know my mom."

"No, I don't." He pulled out his keys, pointed them at the car door, and pressed the unlock button. The car let out a beeping sound. I reached over to open the passenger door but he beat me to it. Before I could give him a look, he laughed. "Geri, just get in the car."

It was a high SUV, which made sense given his size. But when he squeezed into the driver's seat, he looked like he didn't have enough space to move around.

"Have you ever hit your head on the ceiling? Because it's so close to your head?"

He turned the key in the ignition and glanced at me. "I take it you have, in a smaller car? Shorter people don't normally consider these things."

"Maybe once but yeah, it's something I think about."

"My mom learned about this awful tasting Chinese medicine you can drink to make you taller. There might be one to reverse the effects of growth. You know you're still growing, right?"

As someone who didn't want to get any taller, I couldn't help the irritation from tap-dancing across my scalp. "It's okay, I don't need you to do me any favors."

"I'm already doing you a huge one by taking you home." His tone was light, teasing.

"It's not like I asked you to. I could have waited for Helena's driver."

He sighed as he steered us out of the parking lot. "Just give me directions." His voice turned cold. I wanted to tell him I didn't have to be nice to him. Besides, why did I have to worry about how he felt when I knew he was taking me to my doom? But I wasn't made of ice. And I wasn't completely devoid of manners.

"Sorry," I mumbled. "I'm just not looking forward to what's going to meet me when I get home, you know?"

I felt a light punch on my upper arm. I glanced down and saw his paw resting there. "Yeah. If you need any help..."

"If you could convince my mom not to kill me, that would be awesome."

"I don't know about that, but I could help you out with algebra. I'm not too bad at it. We did study that last year."

I looked up at him. "You're in grade 11 then?" I realized I knew next to nothing about him except for the fact that he did aikido and didn't play basketball that well. Oh, and that he knew Matt.

"Yup. And math's easy for me."

"Well, it's like an alien language to me." I looked out the window, chewing on the dry skin on my lower lip. "So what else should I know about you? You apparently know everything about me."

"Not everything."

"How long have you been doing aikido?" Since he was driving, I figured his eyes were on the road so it wasn't rude if I continued to watch the trees and the squat, gray buildings whizz by.

"A few years now."

He wasn't going to make this easy, was he?

"Okay." I dragged the second syllable out to show that I could see what he was doing. "But why aikido and not something else like karate or wushu?"

"Do you really want to know?" His voice had an edge to it and I felt a pang of guilt pinch my gut. "Or are you just asking to pass the time?"

That twinge of guilt morphed into a prickle of annoyance. "Bas, I can be a pain in the butt. I know that. But honestly? If I didn't care about your life, I wouldn't bother asking you questions. I wouldn't even get in the car with you."

"Wow, thanks a lot for doing me the favor."

"No one asked you."

"You know what? Just forget it. Let's stop talking. This isn't working."

I bit my tongue so the angry words in my head wouldn't come out and make the situation even worse. Crossing my arms, I told him, in the least amount of words possible, how to get to my house. When we pulled up outside my front lawn, the grass now longer than it should have been, I mumbled a quick thank you and tugged on the car handle to let myself out.

"Good luck, Geri." It was soft but I heard it. I ducked my head so I could peer at him inside the car, the twilight making it harder to see than usual.

"Thanks." Maybe I was made of ice after all, because I felt it begin to melt away. "For everything."

# Chapter 8

○

"*Naku,* your mom is so angry. Geri, what did you do?" I didn't even get the chance to step through our front door when Yaya Agnes wrapped a plump arm around my waist and shepherded me into our brightly lit kitchen. Just a few years ago, she could put that same arm around my neck. Now, she could no longer reach it without jumping.

She let go of me, bustled over to the refrigerator and pulled out a cake box, talking the whole while about how Ms. Mirasol had called Mom and told her about my algebra situation. Yaya Agnes placed a dessert plate before me as I sat at the kitchen counter. "Eat. I made that this morning."

Yaya Agnes made the best chocolate cake I'd ever tasted in my life, but even the moist, rich goodness with its gooey layer of caramel in the middle didn't ease the knots in my tummy. "I'm going to tell your mom you're here." I didn't bother to stop her. It was going to happen sooner or later. I shoveled the rest of the cake into my mouth and downed it with a glass of water. The kitchen doors swung open and I took a deep breath to steady my hammering heart.

"Geri, tell me what is going on." My mom may be small, but when she was angry, the energy that came off her in what felt like laser-beam accuracy was strong enough to make me want to curl up into a ball of fear and anxiety. She pulled up a light wooden chair next to me and folded her hands on her lap.

"I'm sorry, Mom."

She sat there and stared at me. I wasn't getting off that easy. I launched into what happened on Friday, minus the fight with Simone in the caf. Mom didn't have to know about that. I told her I was giving up basketball and that she didn't have to worry. I ended there, hoping that was enough to get me off the hook. I was wrong.

"Geri, giving up basketball but going to watch a soccer game when you could be studying is not my idea of making an effort." Her voice was quiet. Too quiet. I was definitely in trouble. "You think this isn't serious. You think it's something you can cram at the last minute. But you aren't a child anymore. A few hours isn't enough for you to catch up on what you need to know for the exam." She shut her eyes for a few seconds. "Here's what I don't understand. You always put in the hours when it comes to anything physical. You know your body. You know that it needs time to improve, to learn moves and steps, but when it comes to your brain, you think learning can happen in an instant. Why can't you see they're the same thing?"

She made sense. She did. But what she didn't understand was my heart was not in it. I lived for basketball and ballet because I wanted to get better. I knew what I had to do to hit the goals I set for myself. I could see where I wanted to take myself. When it came to school, especially math, my brain shut down. I didn't see the point of it all. And when that happened, I didn't know where I could dig up the motivation to work on it. Whenever I tried, I came up empty.

"They aren't the same thing, Mom. I love basketball. I love ballet. How can anyone love math?"

Her eyes narrowed and her jaw clenched. "You don't have to love it, Geri! That's not what I'm asking of you. I just want you to try! Just because you don't like it, you automatically give up on it? Is that how you expect to live your life?"

"That's what you and dad did, wasn't it?" The image of my mom started to blur as tears brimmed in my eyes. I stood up, my fists clenched at my sides. "When you didn't want to be around each other anymore, you just gave up! You quit! You quit on our family. On me. On any happiness we could have ever had together."

"No, Geri, that's not what happened."

"Yes, that's what happened! I was there, Mom. I remember everything. Things were fine one day and then the next, he was gone! He was out the door. You got rid of him, didn't you? You got tired of him and kicked him out. So don't tell me that it's wrong to give up on things when I get tired of them. Because you are the best example of that. In fact, all my life that's what you've been teaching me. When something doesn't work, throw it away and find something new, something better. Isn't that right, Mom?"

I stopped when I heard my glass fall to the floor and shatter into a thousand tiny shards. Oh crap. What did I just say to her? I didn't mean it, Mom. I didn't mean any of it. I stared at her with my mouth open, my hand mirroring hers as it flew to my dry lips. Her eyes were as wide as mine, the pain flashing inside them like a pulsing neon sign in bright, blinding colors.

I was the first to look away. I opened my mouth to apologize, to beg for forgiveness, to tell her that wasn't what I believed in my heart. But when I turned my head back to her, she was gone. All I could see was the kitchen door swinging back and forth as if chiding me. *Creak. Creak. Creep. Creep.* That's what you are, Geri. A first-class creep.

My body sagged into the chair I was sitting in earlier, and my head fell into my hands. Where did all that anger come from? Oh, who was I kidding? I was a teenage ball of angst. Everyone knew it. And it would seep out with every word, every action. But the stress and pressure of the past few days were too much for me to keep it bottled up, like a bottle of Coke after a piece of Mentos was tossed into it.

I couldn't leave it this way. I jumped up, tiptoed my way to the small closet next to the fridge and pulled out a dustpan and a broom. The repetitive motion of sweeping up the glass shards soothed the rage in my head, but it also mounted my guilt. I worked up and down the kitchen floor, telling myself I was looking for every last bit of glass. But I knew I was delaying what I needed to do. After pouring the broken pieces into the garbage bin, I tossed my cleaning tools back into the closet and trudged my way up the stairs to Mom's room.

I didn't know what I expected to find, but when I knocked and pushed open her bedroom door, I was surprised to see her sitting on the wooden floor, a photo album open on her lap. She was flipping pages, her fingers brushing her cheek every now and then. I lowered myself next to her and mumbled, "I'm sorry, Mom. I didn't mean what I said."

My heart constricted as I saw what she was looking at. Photos of me, of her, and of my dad. Together. One happy family. She must have hidden these albums when he disappeared.

"I guess I haven't been that honest with you, Geri." Her voice was so soft, I had to lower my head close to her mouth to hear it. My strangled heart began to pound in my chest. "I found your dad a few years ago. I was looking and looking for him, ready to beg him to come back, to talk to me, to drag him to counseling if he agreed. He wasn't easy to find. He cut ties with our common friends, with his family. But I found him."

I couldn't breathe. I knew he left but I thought they both decided to call it quits. I didn't know my mom wanted him to come back. The way I did.

She raised her red-rimmed eyes to mine. "And he refused. I didn't want to tell you because I didn't want you to hate him. I could hate him all I wanted, but he's your dad. Whatever it is, he still deserves some respect, some love from you." Her voice cracked over that hateful four-letter word.

My arms and shoulders grew heavy, as if the weight of what my mom had said was so massive, I couldn't carry it on my own. My spine curled up till I was hugging my knees, protecting the most vulnerable part of my body.

So even if I won the championship, played better than Michael Jordan and Steph Curry combined, my dad would never come back to watch me play. Because he was given the chance and he said no. He didn't want me. It wasn't just Mom he didn't want. He didn't want *me*.

I didn't know I was sobbing till Mom put her arms around me and made shushing noises as if I were a newborn that needed soothing. "He was going through something and needed to work things out for himself. It had nothing to do with you. Nothing to do with us. It took me a while to accept that." Then she took my chin in her hands and lifted my face so I could look into her eyes. "But I need you to know that I tried, Geri. I didn't give up. I wanted to make this work. For you, for me, for our family. I loved your dad. But sometimes, giving up is a way of showing the other person you love them."

I closed my eyes so I didn't have to see the pain in hers, the pain that reflected my own. Pain I had never known the extent and gravity of till that very moment. I took a deep, shuddering breath and swallowed hard. This was something I had to live with. That I wasn't enough to keep my dad at home. And that no matter what I did, he was never coming back.

# Chapter 9

It was the day of the test. While the rumbling air-conditioner blasted arctic air straight at me, Ms. Mirasol was taking her time strolling from desk to desk, handing out a long white sheet of paper. The dreaded questionnaire. When she reached my side, she placed a hand on my shoulder and gave me a look. My gut twisted and I cringed. She expected me to ace this test. Or to at least be ready. Well, I wasn't.

I tapped the eraser of my pencil against my teeth and took a few deep breaths to loosen the knots in my tummy. It wasn't that I didn't study hard. The past few days were all about linear equations, expanding expression, and factorizing. I lived and breathed them. But I had a nagging feeling there was something missing when it came to what I knew. Even Simone seemed to get the process but I just couldn't understand why things computed the way they did.

Two nights ago, while we were sprawled on my bedroom floor, Simone pulled at her short hair and let out a feral howl. All the lights were blazing, including the little orange basketball-shaped nightlight by the bathroom door, and our books were scattered around us amidst balls of crumpled paper (mine because I just wasn't getting this one equation right). "You aren't focusing, Geri!" I could hear the exasperation in her tone. "How can you not understand something I've explained like ten times?"

"I am!" I spluttered, looking up from the pages of her math notebook. I was trying to see if there was anything in there that would make even a little sense to me. "I mean, I get it in the beginning, but as the numbers keep going, and there are other things I should be doing, I get completely lost. Like I have no idea why this is what should be done here!" I shook the notebook at her.

"Because that's just how it should be! Stop looking for reasons and explanations, Geri. Just do what I tell you to do." She grabbed the notebook from me and threw it on the floor. Then in a quiet voice added, "I also told you I'm not good enough to tutor you."

"Sim, there's no one else I want to ask." Bas's offer replayed in my mind but I shook my head to push it out. No thank you, mister.

"I think we need a break. At the very least, I need a break!" She shut the textbook she was holding and stretched her arms above her head. Her eyes widened when they fell on the wall next to my bed. I guess it didn't register earlier when she was so focused on getting me to understand why X had to be transposed in order to be subtracted from Y. Don't ask. I'm just making this up. "Hey, where's Michael?"

I turned my head to face my bare wall, a vertical, dirty-white rectangle marking the spot where Michael Jordan used to hang. I swallowed the thick lump in my throat and remembered what happened that night. After Mom talked to me, I went straight to my room and dove under my bed. I took the three stuffed bears that stood sentinel and tossed them into a big *balikbayan* box. In also went Dad's old gym bag and the gray socks I used to take such good care of.

I stood before Michael for a few minutes, my hands on my hips. I stared at him and wanted to ask if he had known that he was indeed the replacement for my father. Because apparently, I wasn't going to have one anymore. Ever. I stared at the eyes that never looked back at me and felt the deep sting of betrayal skewer my gut. Without allowing myself to think twice, I reached up and peeled the Bulls poster off my wall. The poster that I talked to almost every night, the poster that no longer held the promise of my father's return. Because even if he and I did love the game, that wasn't enough. Because I wasn't enough. And that was fine. As long as I didn't have glaring reminders of it when I opened my eyes in the morning and before I closed them at night. I rolled up the poster and shoved it into the box. I was tempted to rip it apart, but something held me back. I just couldn't bear to destroy what I had pinned my hopes on, even if those hopes were already reduced to pathetic fantasy.

But I wasn't ready to tell Simone any of that. I wasn't exactly raring to announce that my father didn't want me. "I got tired of him. What do you think of putting up Steph Curry instead?"

"I don't know, Ger. He's no Michael Jordan." Simone frowned at me, as if I had committed sacrilege. "But the reigning two-time most valuable player would be better than any ballerina." She smirked.

I made a show of rolling my eyes to the back of my head. "Just for that, I'll put up Roberto Bolle instead. Have you seen him, Sim? He's so hot."

"Who? A guy ballerina? Geri, I don't know about these life choices of yours. They aren't what I would call popular."

"He's a danseur, not a ballerina. You're just saying that because you haven't seen him yet. And my life choices are just unpopular with you!"

"I'm the one who matters, right?"

No. I'm the one who matters. But I didn't tell her that either. I normally would have, but at that moment, I didn't feel like it.

"Yeah, let's get back to that equation." I took a fresh sheet of paper and attempted to solve the same problem for what felt like the twentieth time.

That was how our study sessions went. Simone nearly gave up on me last night, the night before the test, and I almost yelled at her. But we came to our senses when Mom peeked inside my room and asked if we wanted something to eat. It so happened we were just hungry. The food may have soothed our tempers, but it did nothing for my brain. I still understood nothing. So it didn't surprise me that, on the day of reckoning, when I turned my paper around, the number combinations only looked vaguely familiar. I checked my watch to see how many minutes we had left, took a fresh sheet of paper from my bag, and began scribbling whatever I could. Maybe Ms. Mirasol would give me points for getting some parts of the solutions right. Because I doubted my final answers would deliver me from certain tragedy.

# Chapter 10

▽

Even if you know something is bound to happen, when it actually does, you can't help feeling crushed. Maybe I had a smidgeon of hope that I somehow absorbed Simone's understanding of algebra in those few days we were working together. Or maybe I was crossing my fingers that I had managed to awaken something in my brain that switched on my math skills. But no such luck.

That day, after school, I was rushing off to ballet when Ms. Mirasol called out to me in the hall. I had just pulled a short sundress over my tights and leotards. I didn't have access to my basketball jersey and shorts anymore because Mom took them. You'd think she'd trust me not to wear them after I agreed not to play. Or better yet, she should know I didn't need to wear them to play ball. But I was good. I haven't played since. Teacher Justine even allowed me to be absent the past few days so I could study after school. But that meant I had to be early for ballet today because I had to make up for my absences.

"I'm going to ballet, Ms. Mirasol."

"I checked your test first, Geri." She held it in her hands, the test side facing her so I couldn't see the bright red marks, just a faded impression through the paper.

And she called me Geri again. This wasn't good.

"Okay." I swallowed hard, feeling tears begin to prick my eyes. I mean, come on. If it were good news, she wouldn't have come looking for me. She could have just waited to give it in class with the rest of the test papers, right?

She started walking into our classroom, not even looking back to see if I was going to follow. She flicked on the lights, dispelling the gloom all classrooms had when there were no students in them, and sat in one of the chairs. She looked at me, not saying anything. I made myself sit in the chair opposite her and placed my hands on the desk, clasped together. "I failed, didn't I?"

Her gaze softened. "You didn't fail, but you didn't hit 85. So there's still a chance you can pass the year."

I blinked back the tears. A small chance I bet.

"You will most likely fail this quarter though, but if you do well in the next..."

"Ms. Mirasol, how do you expect me to do well in the next quarter? I can't understand anything! Whenever I try solving the problems, I take a wrong turn somewhere and I don't know why!" I was sobbing like a baby. But I didn't care. I had bigger problems to worry about than how pathetic I looked to my algebra teacher. I was going to lose the things I loved. I had already lost the hope that I had a dad who loved me.

"Geri." I felt her put a warm hand on my arm. "I noticed that. Your solutions start out right, but as you keep solving, you make a mistake which leads you down the wrong path and eventually, to the wrong answer."

I held my palms out to her. "So how do I fix that?"

"You need to find a tutor, Geri. I can't tutor you. It goes against school rules. But I can help find you one. As nice as Simone is for helping you out, she is not the best person to teach you algebra." She handed me the paper.

I scanned it, taking note of the red marks, the thin Xs in Ms. Mirasol's neat handwriting, and the big 82 encircled in red at the upper right hand corner. "Three points," I whispered.

"I tried to look for more points to make you hit 85, but I couldn't find any without cheating." My eyes flew up to her face. She could do that?

She gave me a small smile. "I'm not a cold-hearted you-know-what, Geri." Then her face turned serious again. "Why don't you want to hire a tutor? I can speak to your mom about it. I'm sure she—"

"No!" I jumped to my feet, the exam in my hands. "I mean, I can find someone. You don't have to talk to my mom."

"Geri, you do know she will see your report card, right?" Her tone was gentle but I could sense the rebuke in her words.

I shook my head. "I don't plan to hide it from her, miss. I just don't want to bother her with the expense."

"But this is your academic future, Geri. Your mom will find the money."

It was no use explaining to her how much of a financial burden I already was on my mother. "I'll take care of it, miss."

I thought she narrowed her eyes at me but when I blinked, she was nodding her head and getting up. She squeezed my shoulders. "You can do this, Geri. I believe in you. But right now, I have to send a memo to your basketball coach that you're off the team until you pass next quarter."

I wanted to wail about how long that was but another thought clubbed me on the head. Why bother playing when my dad would never care anyway? Even slam-dunking Michael Jordan no longer had a place in my life. I would be fine.

But wait.

"Even ballet?" My vision started to blur. I had to grip the edge of the wooden desk next to me.

Ms. Mirasol's lips stretched into a thin line, the way they did whenever someone in class did something she didn't like. I realized she was preparing herself to say something painful and maybe, just maybe, she was steeling herself against it too. "I'm sorry, Geri. Your grades should come first."

I nodded and stumbled out of the classroom, toward the dismissal gate where Helena was supposed to pick me up and take me to ballet. I saw her sleek, black car parked right by the gate. She was probably inside waiting for me. I wiped my cheeks with the back of my hand as I wobbled over. I raised my hand to knock on the darkly tinted windows when the door flew open.

"Geri, what's wrong?" Helena leapt out, her arms coming around me in a flutter of chiffon.

I clung on to her as Kuya Dex quietly took my bags. "I didn't make it, Hel." I was soaking her chiffon top, but I didn't think she minded.

Her arms tightened around me as she whispered, "Let's get into the car and you can tell me about it." I staggered into the plush seats, never more grateful for my ballet best friend than at that moment.

I had never cried so much in my life. I felt like a leaky faucet without a plumber to tighten whatever pipe needed fixing. The analogy didn't escape me either. My dad being the plumber. So yes, I blamed this all on him. If he hadn't left, if he hadn't abandoned me—actually, no. If he was just freaking sorry for a mistake he had committed seven years ago, I would be willing to forget about the pain. But he didn't even want to acknowledge that, or me. So now my life had gone to crap. Thank you very much, Dad.

These were the thoughts going through my head as I danced through my last ballet class. It took a lot of willpower not to let the tears fall as I practiced my chaînés. But it helped that I had to concentrate on the rapid succession of turns. At the same time, knowing I wasn't going to be part of the recital I had set my heart on conflicted with the drive to do my best. There was a battle waging inside my head: how I should dance my soul out because I didn't know when else I was going to get this chance, but at the same time, why try? Why make the effort?

When Teacher Justine played my solo music, asking me to stand in the center of the studio, my arms in a soft circle close to my body, I shot Helena a panicked look. Not because I didn't know it or didn't want to do it, but because if this was the last time—the last time before an audience no matter how tiny it was—I felt the pressure and most of all, the finality.

Without bothering to wipe the tears that were now falling onto my cheeks, I lifted myself on my toes, held my arms over my head, brought my leg straight up behind me as high as it could go, spun around, and leapt in the air. If this was it, then I was going to give the performance of my life. In this dingy studio that doubled as a dojo, one that needed scented candles to diffuse the smell of dirty gym socks, one with only my teacher and six of my classmates to watch me. Because I didn't need the stage or the lights or the VIPs in the audience. Not if this was going to be the last time I danced in a long time.

When I curtseyed to my classmates as the music ended, my chest heaving from the strain of crying while dancing my heart out, Helena ran to hug me, tears streaming down her cheeks as well.

When she tightened her arms around my neck, she breathed, "You'll survive this, Geri. You will dance on stage again. Even if it's not in our recital."

My classmates came to hug me too, the news spreading as if I had tweeted it to them. Which, you've got to admit, is a lot quicker than a game of verbal pass the message. Teacher Justine approached, handing me a box of tissue. The girls cleared a spot for her but still stayed close enough to hear every word.

"Will you tell us what's wrong, Geri?" she asked, her hands folding together before her.

I swallowed, took a deep breath, and launched into my story. I kept it short. I didn't want to take up even more class time. When she nodded, put her hands on my shoulders and squeezed them tight, I bit my lip in worry. Was she going to reprimand me too?

"Geri, you know that dance will always be here for you."

I heard my classmates collectively sigh in relief. I was pretty sure they were imagining themselves in my shoes.

"I believe you'll be able to sort out your academics." She looked me in the eye and I tried not to flinch at the seriousness of her stare. "Because I know that's how much ballet means to you." Then her face softened and she pulled me into her arms. I hugged her tight and whispered a thank you.

After class, I waited for everyone to leave before thanking Teacher Justine again for her reassuring words. When I yanked the door open, I stumbled into Bas. He was blocking the doorway like a pillar of white cloth with a black belt around his waist. I almost tripped over my feet as I backed up to avoid ramming into him. He reached out an arm to steady me and when I mumbled a hurried thanks, he stepped closer, blocking my way out. "You're crying."

"Not anymore."

"Your eyes are puffy and your nose is red."

"Thanks a lot. Any girl would love to be complimented that way." I tried to get past him by attempting to fit myself in between his bulk and the wall. But he wasn't letting me go, apparently. He stepped to the right and peered down at me.

I glowered at him, my hands flying to his shoulders, ready to push with all my might. Even if I knew that wasn't going to do any good.

"You do know I regularly train to grab those hands and twist till I can flip my opponent onto his stomach. Or in this case, *her* stomach."

I yanked my hands back as quickly as if they were attached to a stretched out rubber band. "You wouldn't dare."

His face split open into a grin. "No, not like this anyway. In the dojo, yes." Then he put his hand on my shoulder. "Talk to me, Geri. What's going on?"

I wanted to bury my face in my hands, embarrassed at how I had treated him when we were last together. Instead, I pointed at the wall outside the studio and we both slid down to the floor. I pulled my knees up and rested my arms on them. I forced my lips up into a smile, probably looking gruesome with my red face, but I saw him return my attempt with one of his own. His eyes dipped down at the sides again. And the guilt gnawed at my gut. "Don't you hate me?" I gave a small laugh.

His smile turned into a smirk. "Yeah, most of the time." Then it softened. "But not today."

"I didn't make the grade. So I'm off the team, out of the recital, and that was my last ballet class." I kept my eyes on my scuffed white sneaks. I didn't think I'd miss my basketball shoes this much.

"Well, you danced like it was." Pause. "And before you bite my head off, I meant that in a good way. I thought your last solo was awesome. But this one..."

I couldn't help it, I burst out laughing. "Oh geez, am I that horrible to you?"

He nudged my shoulder with his arm, since our shoulders didn't exactly align. "I think I'm getting used to it."

"Thanks. For what you said about my dancing."

An awkward silence followed, but I wasn't going to be the first one to break it.

"So do you have a plan? Can I ask that?"

"You just asked it. Can't take it back now."

"And that's why I asked. I can never tell when something is going to annoy you."

I pressed my lips together to keep the snort from escaping. I jumped to my feet and looked down at him sitting on the floor, his long beefy limbs taking up so much space. "I was about to call my mom to pick me up already—"

"I can take you home."

"I wasn't going to ask you that, but okay, thanks." I chewed on my lower lip. "I was going to ask if you wanted to get a mango shake across the street." After the day I had, I needed something to make me feel better. And just the thought of crushed ice and fresh mangoes blended together with lots of syrup was enough to make my mouth water.

I watched Bas get to his feet. I couldn't fathom how someone so huge could move as if he weighed less than I did. In about two seconds, he was out the door, leaving me to chase after him, my hands tight around my backpack straps. When I finally caught up with him outside the building, he glanced at me. "It closes in ten minutes. You should have told me you wanted a shake earlier!"

My mouth fell open. "It what?" I took off and yelled, "So why aren't you running?"

I heard his laughter behind me but I didn't stop till I got to the fruit juice stall across the street. Glad the quick sprint didn't leave me out of breath, I asked the *kuya* behind the booth for two mango shakes. I leaned on the counter as Bas approached. He wasn't that far behind, but I was happy to note that I was faster than him.

"Why do I feel like I lost a race I didn't join?" He wasn't out of breath either. Points for Dojo guy.

"Because you just did."

"Is everything a competition with you?"

"No." Then I remembered our game of one-on-one. "Maybe."

He leaned against the counter next to me. "I take that as a yes."

When the *kuya* handed us our shakes, I dug into my pocket and thrust the bills at him. "It's on me. For...the grief I'm always causing you."

He raised his eyebrows. "That almost makes me forgive each and every rude thing you've said to me. Almost." Then he took a sip of his shake through the striped paper straw and closed his eyes. "Well, that changes things."

I poked him in the tummy, my finger retracting at how hard it was. What did I expect? Flab above that black belt? "Explain."

He pushed the paper cup in my hands up to my mouth. "Taste it and you tell me."

I closed my lips around the paper straw and the icy sweetness filled my mouth. "Wow, Kuya, what did you put in this thing?"

The *kuya* smiled at me. I thanked him and we began walking back to the studio, sipping our shakes. I could tell the mangoes were naturally sweet and it wasn't just the syrup that gave the drink flavor. At this time of year, the rainy season, mangoes were sour and I was used to a sharp tang in my usually sweet shake. But this one.

"They probably have a magic farm or something. I love the shakes there." Bas still had his straw in his mouth while he talked.

"This is the first one I've had. I see the stall on my way to ballet, but I never felt I deserved a mango shake as much as I did today." I jumped into a pile of damp leaves, listening to them squish.

We sat on the same short, wooden bench right outside the building entrance and continued to drink our shakes in silence. This time, I was the first to break it. Not because it was an uncomfortable silence, but because I remembered something I really wanted to ask him. "How do you know Matt?"

Bas tilted his head to look at me, his lips still around the straw. He seemed to be weighing his words before speaking them out loud. Finally, he lowered the shake. "He was my mentor."

"Your what?"

"Years ago, I was what my school liked to call a troubled kid."

"You?" It was then that I realized my image of him was the complete opposite of me. A guy who followed the rules, studied hard, did aikido—the least competitive martial art—, yeah, I kinda looked it up, so what?—and did everything right. He didn't even call me out when I was being a brat. So yeah, hearing that was a surprise. It was also surprising how I pieced together a character sketch of him without even knowing him that well.

"Yeah, I was angry, I didn't have an outlet or a way to express my anger so I..." He squinted at me and took a breath. "I bullied the smaller kids."

"You used your bulk to intimidate them?" I wanted to tease him but I could sense the heaviness of his words, as if he were confessing something to me. And a part of me felt touched, honored to be on the receiving end of something so personal.

All I wanted to know was how he knew Matt, but I guess it wasn't a simple answer. Or maybe I had crossed into the realm of friend. I held my tongue and waited.

"Yeah. Sort of. I sensed which kids were easily scared and just pushed them a bit more. It wasn't my proudest moment." He bent his head. I wanted to reach out and run my hand across it but that would have been way too familiar. So I put my empty cup down on the ground and sat on my hands instead. They were cold from holding the shake and needed warming anyway.

"The school stepped in, with all sorts of discussions, counseling, and therapy," he continued. "But I was just getting angrier and angrier. In the end, they enrolled me in this mentorship program where I hung out with a guy older than me, played sports with him, and finally, he took me to my first aikido session. I owe Matt my sanity."

Were we talking about the same Matt? My mom's boyfriend? The one I thought was a shallow, food-loving moron who my friends had crushes on?

"He told me aikido was the best way to calm myself down, sort out my anger issues. He practiced it too but not as obsessively as I do now. But he introduced it to me and I'll always be grateful to him for that." He gave me a small smile, which I tried to return, while still trying to process this new information about Bas and Matt.

"Has..." I licked my lips, terrified of the answer. "Has Matt said anything about me?"

"He's told me about your mom, how she's awesome and how he loves her so much. And that she has a daughter about my age who plays amazing basketball. I don't think he's seen you dance though. He's never mentioned that to me."

I swallowed, the guilt now moving up from my gut to my heart. "No, I've never invited him to watch me dance. He's only seen me play because Mom didn't tell me he was coming. I was really pissed off that he was there." Did I just admit *that* to him? After he told me this guy changed his life? Saved his sanity?

But Bas didn't look angry. In fact, he looked amused. "You make his life a living hell, don't you?"

I opened my mouth, about to defend myself. But when he grinned, I felt the hot air rush out of my balloon of bravado. "Yeah. I do."

"I wouldn't expect anything less from you, Geri." He laughed. "But Matt's a good guy. I promise. And he really loves your mom."

"I know that." I groaned. "But I can't stand that he's there to take my dad's place, you know? And he tries so freaking hard." I covered my face with my hands. "But now, I might as well have no dad."

I felt his hand on my shoulder. His touch was light, tentative, as if he were afraid I would break if he put more pressure. "Because?"

I didn't want to cry anymore. I was tired of it. I tried to keep the words in, but when I lifted my face from my hands and glanced up at Bas, it seemed as if he knew what I was talking about. So out came the story. The story I didn't even tell Helena or Simone. The story about how my dad didn't want me, how he had been given the chance but still said no. How I was such a brat when it came to Matt but he was apparently the one who deserved my respect. How I was hanging on to the wrong man.

"Dads can be jerks." His eyes were on the ground when he said that.

*Yes.* But I let him continue.

"That episode in my life? When I was 'troubled?'" He put the word in air quotes. "It was because of my dad. I had just found out that my biological dad wasn't the dad I knew. He wasn't the guy I lived with, grew up with. My mom had gotten pregnant and my real dad didn't want to have anything to do with me. When she told me, she even showed me photos of him on Facebook. I saw him with his other family, kids who looked just like me. I even met them. We played bowling. I beat them all, but in the end, I felt like the loser. Because while I waited for Mom to pick me up, they all went home together. One big, happy family. So I lashed out. Against my mom, against my stepdad, against my half-siblings. So yeah, I know what that's like."

I couldn't breathe. And when I looked down at my hands, they were clutching his. I wasn't even aware I had grabbed on to them while he was talking. "You met him? You met his other family? Have you seen them again since?"

He smiled and squeezed my hands, not letting go. "Yeah. It's a lot better now. We actually get along. They're cool kids. The youngest one, Sherry, wants to do aikido with me. I told her to convince our dad."

"I can't imagine that." I looked away, at the trees dotting the sidewalk, at the now graying sky. "What if my dad has other kids? What if that's why he doesn't want to see me?"

I felt his hand on my cheek as he turned my face to his. "He probably had a reason for not wanting to see you. Whatever crap reason it is, he must have thought it was a good one at the time."

"I don't know if I'll be able to handle it if he has another family."

"You're already handling yourself so well, Geri. You're not beating up little kids, you dance like you're on air, and you play like you're on fire."

I swallowed. "But I'm angry. I'm so angry all the time, Bas."

"I know. I was like that too. I'd ask you to join an aikido class, but..."

I shook my head, letting go of his hands. "But yeah, I need to study. Why does my life suck so much?"

"It doesn't have to." His voice was so soft, I almost couldn't catch it. I blinked, my mind clearing. I had just spilled my guts to this guy and I didn't hate him or myself. I looked at him, surprised that we weren't fighting, that I wasn't embarrassed. I almost threw my arms around him but that would definitely have embarrassed me.

I took a deep breath and asked, my heart pounding in my chest, "Will you help me, Bas?" I felt the heat creep up my cheeks and spread to my scalp. "Will you help me with math? I need to dance again. I need to play ball again. And I can't allow myself to become even more troubled than I already am."

He smiled and pulled me to him in an embrace that almost cut off my circulation. Then I heard him murmur close to my ear, "I thought you'd never ask."

# Chapter 11

Telling my mom about my grades wasn't as mortifying as I thought it would be. While in Bas's car, I called to tell her he was taking me home and to give her the news. I quickly slipped in that I had asked Bas to tutor me and he didn't want me to pay him. Maybe that softened the blow or gave her hope that I wasn't going to be a total failure. I told her he just wanted me to pull my grades up as quickly as possible so we could dance in his aikido exhibition together. She said she was going to put in a few more hours at work since I didn't need a ride home anymore and that we could talk about it some more later. But she didn't sound upset and that was one thing to be grateful for. After that talk we had about my dad, things had been a little strained between us. She wasn't mad, she was just more careful around me and I didn't like that. I wanted things back to normal. Back to not knowing my dad was a total dirt bag.

"What if we study for the first hour, then practice our performance the hour after that?" Bas stood outside my front door after taking me home.

I wrinkled my nose when he started talking to me about the exhibition. I know I said I'd do it, but right now, I felt I had more important things to focus on. And we didn't exactly have a lot of time either. The exhibition was in two weeks. "Okay." I shrugged.

"Come on! Fake some enthusiasm, Geri."

I dropped my bags and threw my hands on the grass, doing two cartwheels in a row. "Happy now? Bet you can't do that."

"Yeah, definitely not competitive." He joined me on the grass fronting our house, backed up a few paces, and began to run toward me. He dove headfirst and did a flip in the air without using his hands.

I crossed my arms over my chest as I walked back to our front door. "I can see it now. A harmonious working relationship indeed."

"Hey, I didn't start it!" He jogged over to me, pulling down his shirt which had crept up a bit while he did his somersault. A part of me wished it had moved up even higher so I could see just how well defined that hard stomach was. I spun away from him and rang the doorbell, hoping he couldn't read my thoughts.

The door opened to Matt's beaming face. "Geri! Bas! It's great to see you guys!"

I bit my tongue when they gave each other a hug. I was about to ask what Matt was doing there that early, but I reminded myself about what Bas had told me. That he was the good guy. He still annoyed me though.

"We're here to study." Bas told Matt as we entered the living room. I noticed there was a half-eaten sandwich on the coffee table in front of our TV, and some show I didn't recognize was on.

"We can stay in the kitchen." I kicked the swinging door open to get away from Matt, but he followed us in, greeting Yaya Agnes with a warm smile. I caught her blush and shook my head at her betrayal.

"Yaya Agnes made me a strawberry shake. You guys might want one too. I brought fresh strawberries down from Baguio." I didn't even know he went to Baguio.

"But they aren't in season." I frowned. I know. Killjoy. It was automatic especially when it came to him.

"That's why I put lots of sugar!" Yaya Agnes put two tall, sweaty glasses in front of me and Bas.

I nodded my head as I took a sip. "This is good. Not as good as the mango shake we just had but good."

"You already had shakes?" Matt's handsome face fell as he pulled up a chair and turned it around so he could straddle it. "And here I thought I was offering you something special."

I was about to roll my eyes when I caught Bas looking at me as if telling me to cool it. I sighed and said, "Thank you, Matt."

When his eyebrows shot up, I didn't know if I was going to laugh or cover my face in embarrassment and guilt. Bas saved me from doing either by settling into a chair next to Matt's and digging my algebra book out of my bag.

"Hey! Who said you could touch my things?" I was about to grab my bag when he tossed it to me. I caught it and hugged it to my chest.

"I need to see your book. Figure out where to begin. It's not like I do this for a living, you know." He didn't even look ashamed. He began flipping pages and scanning them while I put down my bag and sat next to him.

"You're helping Geri with math?" Matt asked, his eyes alert, interested. The way they always were. He reminded me of a preschooler listening to a favorite story.

Bas nodded. "It's the only way she agreed to dance with me."

"She's going as your date to the dance?"

"What? No!" I blurted out.

Both sets of eyes turned to me. One pair looked amused while the other...I wasn't sure what his eyes looked like because Bas quickly put his head back down and continued reading my textbook. But the need to explain overcame me. "I mean, that's not it. Bas asked me to dance while he does his aikido exhibition."

Matt tilted his head. "That sounds interesting."

"You want to come?" Bas looked up again. I kicked him under the table and he shot me another look.

"I'd love to. Just let me know when." As if he had already gotten what he came for, Matt stood and put his hand on Bas's shoulder. "I'll leave you guys to it. Good luck, Geri. I'll be in the living room if you need me."

When the door swung shut and I was sure Yaya Agnes was no longer in the kitchen, I muttered, "I tried, okay?"

"Well, you have to try harder. It was painful to witness that." Bas glowered at me.

"I'm usually much worse." It wasn't something to be proud of.

"Matt must really love your mom to put up with you then." Before I could say something in my defense, Bas tore two sheets of paper from the pad next to him and shoved the textbook at me. "Here. Answer these numbers. Use this as your scratch paper and this as your answer sheet." Then he folded the scratch paper into three columns and drew vertical lines to divide them. "Be neat when you use the scratch paper. That really helps when I solve stuff. I used to just write wherever there was space but that confused the hell out of me."

Determined to prove I wasn't an idiot, I took the sheets of paper and my textbook and forced my brain into submission. After a few minutes, I put the pages in front of him. He was leaning forward in his chair, sketching something. "Don't you have anything to study?" I hated it when I was working so hard and the people around me were just slacking off. Not that he was slacking off, he was helping me with my math after all.

"I'm trying to figure out our moves. Thought it would help if I drew my ideas." He lifted the arm that was blocking my view and I was able to get a good look at his drawings. I reached over and took the sheet from the table. Though his sketches weren't exactly works of art, I could tell what movements he wanted us to do.

"This is great. I can already imagine them!"

But he wasn't listening. His brow was furrowed as his pencil flew across my paper, jotting down numbers alongside mine. I peered over his arm to see him crossing things out and encircling others. My stomach plummeted at how many mistakes I made, but I told myself now was not the time to compete against him. I was here to learn. And I couldn't do that if I was going to let my pride get in the way.

When he finally lifted his head and put the paper in front of me, I was ready. I listened to him point out where I went wrong, what I needed to work on, and how to get the answers right. It took me two tries and another strawberry shake, but I was finally able to solve them on my own. When he grinned and raised his hand for a high-five, I jumped out of my chair and did a pirouette right there in the kitchen, in my sneakers. "Bas, no one has ever explained it to me that way." I smiled when I landed on both feet. "Thank you."

"You're welcome." He did a little bow, reminding me of when we first met and argued over who got dibs on the studio. I got a strange ache in my chest when I thought of how different things were between us now, yet funnily enough, still the same. "Now let's practice!" He took the sheet of paper with his sketches and looked around the kitchen. "Are we going to do this here? I don't think we have enough room."

I grinned, closed my hand around his wrist and pulled him out into the front lawn. "I think we'll have more space out there."

Matt looked up from his show when we passed him on our way out. Bas gave him a salute and mouthed something I didn't catch. Matt nodded and slumped back down, his eyes on the screen once more. I was glad he wasn't going to go out and watch us. I wouldn't have been able to concentrate if I had to be nice to him as well as work on an aikido-ballet combination I wasn't even sure was possible.

Bas put the sheet of paper down on the grass and faced me. "Okay, I was thinking we practice some of the combinations I thought up. I'm just basing yours on what I've seen on YouTube."

"Wait, Bas, what if we do a story? Ballet usually has a narrative." As I watched him watch me, an idea bounced into my brain. "Maybe we can do *Camelot*! What do you think?"

"You Lancelot, me Guinevere?" He grinned.

"Yes. Do you have a problem with that?"

He burst out laughing. "Fine. I asked for that. But I like it. Let's choose a scene."

"I actually want to do the part where they meet for the first time. Arthur and Guinevere. We can do huge movements since he's telling her about Camelot. And I can dance the questions. We can take turns that way. Then in the end, we can do something together. Have you thought about lifting me?" My heart pounded at the thought and I wasn't sure why. Maybe too much sugar from all those shakes.

"I don't think that would be a problem." Despite what he said, he sounded a bit uncertain. Or was he just uncomfortable?

"Well, what did you think we'd be doing together? We can't just take turns. Why bother then?" My hands flew into the air.

He approached me as if in slow motion, his eyes on mine. The uncertainty was replaced with determination. I gulped. He wasn't going to throw me to the ground, was he? I jumped when he took my hand.

"I was thinking something more like this." He placed my hand over his and with his other hand, twisted our wrists. "Turn my hand this way and I'll flip. Then you can move your arms around your head the way you did earlier—"

"Like this?" Trying to distract myself from being so close to him and actually touching his skin, I made sweeping arcs over my head with my right arm.

"Yes, like that!" He grinned at me. I nodded, still hyperaware of our skin in contact. "Let's try it."

I put my hand on his warm wrist, thinking this was a horrible idea. How was I going to concentrate on anything when I was so affected by his touch? When I twisted and he flipped, his legs slicing through the air like a fan, I swept the air with my arm. I had to admit it looked good. I added a slight leap with both legs scissoring in the breeze.

Bas's grin was infectious. "This is great, Geri! Let's try a few more. I'll begin an aikido move then you answer with a ballet move."

We continued that way for a few minutes till we were able to pinpoint which combos we wanted to keep and which ones didn't work. I could feel the sweat on my brow and back and I was about to go into the house and get us glasses of water when Matt came out with a jug.

"I was watching you guys from the window and it's looking good." He handed the jug to me and I took a swig before giving it to Bas.

"Thanks," I mumbled.

"It's all Geri." Bas nodded at me, wiping his mouth with the back of his hand. He glanced at his watch and his hand flew up to clutch his head. "Oh no, I've got to head home! My mom's going to kill me. I forgot to tell her I was coming here." He gave Matt a one-armed hug and started in my direction but stopped before he could get any closer. He raised his hand in a little wave instead and handed the jug to me. "See you tomorrow? I don't have aikido so we can work on math right after school."

I wanted to ask why he stopped, where my hug was. But let's face it. He was probably afraid of what I'd do or say. "Yeah, tomorrow. Thanks, Bas." I lifted my hand to wave back, not quite sure why the disappointment weighed so heavily on my shoulders.

As we watched Bas drive away, Matt, his hands in his pockets, said, "I think it's great you guys are friends."

I swallowed, my hands still around the jug Bas handed me. I took another drink and felt something lift together with my thirst. A little shard of darkness in my heart, perhaps? I sat down on the grass, looked up at Matt, and bent my head toward the space next to me. Something flickered in his eyes, but nothing on his face betrayed the surprise he probably felt. When he sat beside me, I said, "What's really great is what you did for him, Matt."

"He told you about that? Last year, he wouldn't have told anybody what he was going through."

"Well, I kinda started it." I gulped, plunging headlong into this new level of trust I was offering him. I felt a little dizzy as the words spilled out of me. "I told him about my dad." My voice cracked. I couldn't believe I was talking to Matt about my dad. It felt worse than a betrayal, but at the same time, I felt like those cartoon animals who inhaled too much air. They blew up, up, up till they began to float. Then they began to fly.

"He told me about his dad too. It gave me hope, you know? But it also made me see that I've been the worst kind of person to you. I..." I took a deep breath, my hands shaking, my voice quivering. "I'm so sorry, Matt."

"I am dying to hug you right now, but you might just take everything back." His face beamed. And were those tears in his eyes? Crap, Matt. I was barely holding it together as it was.

I snorted instead. "I just might. Keep your distance."

He laughed then sobered up. "But Bas didn't tell you the whole story. He thinks I'm some sort of hero who was helping kids out of the goodness of my heart. That's not really how it went down."

Oh great. Here it was. The confession that was going to make me hate men all over again. Just when I was starting to think guys didn't suck after all.

"I joined the mentorship program because I was getting over a bad breakup. I had difficulty moving on and a friend told me that if I helped other people, I might forget about what a loser I was." He grimaced, but I was relieved that was all it was. "So it started as a selfish thing. In the beginning, I wasn't even focused on Bas's problems. I took him out and we hardly talked. We just played whatever sport we could. Then a few weeks into it, I realized he was a living, breathing being with bigger problems than I had. That's when I started to get to know him, that's when I forgot about myself and my self-pity. So in a way, he saved me as much as he claims I saved him."

"A regular bromance. I should warn Mom about this." My tone was still snarky, but because we weren't on the same plane of animosity anymore—or at least, I wasn't—Matt chuckled.

"Well, it looks like that might change pretty soon and give way to another kind of romance."

"What do you—do you mean me and Bas?" Where did he get that idea? Was he talking to my friends?

He shrugged but his expression did not look innocent at all. "I might be off the mark, but I sense something between you two."

A loud revving sound startled me out of my indignation. Mom was pulling up next to the sidewalk. Matt got to his feet in an easy, fluid motion and hastened to the car. I usually turned away when I saw them show any sign of affection for each other. But this time, I noticed how my mom jumped out and leaned into him a little bit before giving him a light peck on the lips. I wasn't grossed out. They were never all over each other and I truly appreciated that—no matter what kind of nasty comments I made about them. What I did notice again and again was how my mother brightened up whenever Matt was around. Like a drooping flower that had just been sprinkled with a little bit of rain. And now that I could see it without resenting every move he made, I realized Matt hadn't just saved one life from despair, he'd actually saved two.

# Chapter 12

For the next few days, I focused on math and our aikido dance—or whatever Bas was calling it. Since I was off the basketball team and no longer in ballet class, I headed straight home after school, sometimes catching a ride with Simone, sometimes being picked up by Mom. She would leave me and Bas alone in the kitchen while Yaya Agnes hovered, refilling our glasses of juice or plopping down more food in front of us. Because I wasn't training or dancing anymore, I didn't want to eat as much as I used to. If I gained weight, it was going to be so much harder for me to move once I finally beat the algebra beast. But Bas and Yaya Agnes were making it frustratingly difficult. He always stuffed his face like it was his last meal ever, making me feel like I was depriving myself if I just had one slice of bread instead of three. But the worst part was when he dangled food in front of my face. Like the cinnamon-sprinkled donut he was now waving back and forth near my mouth. So I opened wide and took a bite.

"Hey, that was my donut!"

"What did you expect me to do?" My mouth was still full when I answered him.

"Get your own, for one." He shoved the rest into his mouth and took another donut from the plate. "I had a rough day. I didn't like my packed lunch and I ran out of money so I couldn't get anything in the caf."

"Oh, you poor thing. So you just wasted the food that was prepared for you and starved instead?"

"Of course not! I ate it all. But I wasn't happy."

I snorted. Food was a big deal to him. And of course Yaya Agnes heard this and brought out a rectangular glass dish filled with her cheesy, meaty lasagna, the top layer a golden shade of brown still glistening after baking in the oven. She put it in front of Bas then scurried off to get plates and forks.

"Was this supposed to be our dinner?" I gaped. I mean, I owed the guy a lot but come on, he was just like Matt, eating all our food! What was *I* going to eat later?

Yaya clucked at me. "Of course not. I made this for Bas's *merienda*."

"Oh really. For Bas and not for me. Because he's the only one who studies here in the afternoons." I made a face at her.

"Geri! You know that's not what I meant. It's for you also." She tapped me on the head, smiling.

I raised my hands to the ceiling. "What to do to get any love around here?"

"Well, you can stop biting other people's donuts." Bas grumbled next to me.

I swatted him on the arm. "They're *my* donuts. Or at least, I think they are. Yaya Agnes might say she bought them for you too." Realizing that could actually be true, I changed the subject. "So I have a test on Thursday."

"That's great!" Why did he look so excited about this? I was terrified. "You can finally prove to everyone that you know this stuff!"

"Who says I know this stuff? I can only get it right after you explain what I did wrong!" I could feel the panic coiling around my neck like a boa constrictor about to strike.

He took my hands and squeezed them. "Geri, look at me. Now take a deep breath. We will prepare for this test. But you also have to know that you're doing so much better. Can't you see it?"

I closed my eyes. "Maybe. I'm just afraid that when I see all those new numbers, I won't have a single idea what to do with them." I squeezed his hands back. I liked how warm and comforting they felt around mine.

"Let's stop working on the dance first and just concentrate on this test. Then when you ace it—and I promise you will because I'm just that good a tutor—I'll let you beat me in basketball again."

I opened my eyes in time to catch his smirk. "Hah! That's nothing. I will always beat you in basketball." I let go of his hands. It would have been too weird if we just held on like that forever. Though that didn't seem like such a horrible thought. I could think of worse things.

"Fine, a prize then. What do you want?"

Ooh. I never really thought in terms of rewards. My mom wasn't big on them because we couldn't afford to spend on things that weren't in the budget. At least after Dad had left. I blinked when Bas waved a hand in front of my eyes.

"You disappeared for a second. Where did you go?"

I grimaced. "Sorry, I was thinking of my dad."

"Tell you what. I was actually saving this for a special occasion, but..." He turned away and bent over to fish something out of his backpack. The words "special occasion" played over and over in my head. What was this about? I felt the warmth heighten in my cheeks. "Here they are!" He waved two yellow strips of board paper in the air. My heart stopped. I knew what those were. I dove to grab them from him.

"Bas! Are these for me?" I snatched them from his hands,

my eyes greedy as they drank in the bold, black letters that spelled out *Sleeping Beauty, The Ballet.*

"My cousin works for their public relations company and she was giving away tickets so of course I told her I had a friend who would love to—"

"Wait, but these are only if I ace the test, right?" I lowered the tickets to the table.

"Now they are."

"I hate you!"

"Isn't that motivation?" His smile was maddening.

I took a deep breath and growled at him. "I will ace this test. And I will watch *Sleeping Beauty.*"

"With me?"

"Are you serious? You want to watch this? Most guys wouldn't even—"

"It's important to you. Of course I want to watch it with you."

My forehead wrinkled at the sudden shift in his tone. And I felt my mouth go dry. I looked down at my textbook, all my words flying out of my head. I put the tickets in front of him and nodded. I couldn't seem to do anything else.

"Then let's make it happen." His eyes crinkled up at the sides.

I flipped open my math notebook and began writing down the equations I needed to solve. While Bas read something for his English class, I put my head down and tried to remember everything I had learned over the past few days. Bas was right though, I was seeing the numbers differently now. Instead of being intimidated and thinking they were out to trick me, I saw them as puzzle pieces that already had solutions. I just needed the right tools to solve them, and those tools were all in my head, waiting for me to pull them out at the right time.

When I had gotten to the last number, I reviewed my answers and slapped my notebook down in front of Bas.

"I'm done!" I jumped up and stretched my arms above my head. "I've been wanting to catch this performance of *Sleeping Beauty*. The principal ballerina is from Cebu, the one who competed in Russia and Bulgaria. I saw something about it on Facebook but I..."

He looked up from my notebook when I trailed off, his eyes darker than usual. "But you?"

"I didn't want to bother my mom with the additional expense."

A sad look crossed his features, then he grinned. "Well that just means you need to win this bet, right?"

"Who said it was a bet? This is my prize. And I will deserve it." I skipped around to his side of the table and leaned on him as he studied my answers. I was hoping I could tip him over. I had so much nervous energy coursing through me like an electric current—from answering all those equations to the possibility of watching *Sleeping Beauty*—and I needed to dispel some of it. When he didn't budge, I put even more force into it, pushing on the floor with my foot. "Hurry up! Aren't you done checking yet?"

"Are you trying to distract me so I won't see which numbers you got wrong? Your answers on this exercise have no bearing whatsoever on whether you get the tickets or not." He raised his head, giving me a bored look.

"You're taking too long! And you're like a rock." I leaned back then tried to ram him with my bicep. The next thing I knew, his arms were around me and he was lifting me on to his shoulder as if I were a sack of rice or a caveman's bride. I didn't know which was worse. He marched into the living room, stopped in front of the TV, and leaned forward so I tumbled onto the sofa.

"What on earth?" I spluttered, pushing my hair away from my face.

"You are bothering me." And he marched back into the kitchen.

I straightened up and almost jumped three feet in the air when I saw my mom standing by the stairs, holding her laptop and a glass of water. She had a funny look on her face. "Hmm. Now I know what to do when you aren't obeying me. I should have asked for parenting advice from that boy earlier."

I pushed myself up and laughed. "I don't think you can carry me, Mom. You're a shrimp."

She put her glass and laptop down on the coffee table and sat next to me. "It would have been a good idea a few years ago when I could still carry you. Are you doing okay?"

I nodded and told her about my test. And about Bas's prize.

"I knew there was something special about that boy." Her eyes twinkled.

"Whatever, Mom." I hauled myself up and headed back to the kitchen. Before I pushed the door open, I felt a smile dance around my lips. Even if I would never admit it to her, she may actually be right.

~~~

Day of the test. I was ready. I was pumped. The butterflies in my tummy were holding a ballet recital and a basketball tournament at the same time.

"You gonna be okay, Ger?" Simone poked me in the side, her eyebrows riding low on her forehead. I didn't think she blamed herself for my last exam, but since then, she would often ask me if I was doing okay, if I understood our new lessons. I did tell her I was getting help, I just didn't say who was helping me. I wasn't ready for the teasing. Because I knew I was going to get a lot of it and I had enough to worry about.

I gave her a quivery smile. "I have no idea, but here we go." I faced forward and took a deep breath, hoping that would settle the butterflies down.

When Ms. Mirasol handed out the papers, she tapped me on the shoulder again. I liked to think it was for luck. I bent my head over the test and scanned the numbers. I was prepared for the sinking dread to settle at the bottom of my belly when I realized I actually knew how to solve the first number. I moved on to the next and the dread began to dissipate with each equation. I wanted to leap to my feet and cartwheel all over the classroom. I had never felt this way while taking a math test before. I mean, sure, I used to think that maybe I could solve a math problem this way or that way and I tried whatever worked, but I never had this confidence. This certainty. I took my scratch paper, which I had divided into three columns the way Bas had taught me and started with number one.

When I finished everything, reviewed my answers, and felt with all the conviction in my heart that I had not only done my best, but that my best had indeed leveled up quite a few notches, I stood up and handed my paper to Ms. Mirasol. She lifted an eyebrow and I gave her a small smile, one that was ready to burst into a beam. Even if I didn't get everything right, this was the first time I had taken a math test and felt this kind of assurance.

After the test, Simone and I found ourselves in the caf together with other girls from the basketball team. They were telling me about Coach's latest drill. It was a combination of burpees, sprints, and free weights. I couldn't believe I found myself missing something I used to hate so much.

"But Geri is going to pass next quarter and she's going to be back before the season starts," Simone announced, lifting a shriveled up siomai with a toothpick and sliding it into her mouth.

Mathilde, the girl to my left, who was two batches lower, had her forehead all scrunched up. "Is math going to get that much harder? I'm already struggling as it is."

"Just don't get me as a tutor." Simone laughed, elbowing me in the ribs.

I took a swig from my water bottle before answering. "I didn't fail, Sim. I just didn't get the grade Ms. Mirasol said I needed. So if Mathilde isn't that behind, you can actually tutor her."

Simone shook her head. "No way. I only did that for you, Geri. My tutoring days are over."

"Or you can always ask the guy tutoring Geri," Denise, the girl across from me chirped. I glanced at her, trying to read her expression, but she wasn't giving anything away.

"Who is tutoring you anyway? You never said." Simone turned her body to face me. This wasn't supposed to be an interesting topic. The team wasn't supposed to care about stuff like this. But I saw every pair of eyes at that table trained on me, waiting for me to answer. And the longer I took, the higher their eyebrows went.

"Bas Mercado."

"Who?"

"That cute guy at the soccer game!"

"The big one?"

"Yeah, Simone says he does aikido."

"Is that like judo?"

"Who cares? He's cute."

"Does she like him?"

"Does he like her?"

"Wait, wait! Why do you guys know so much about him?" I held up my hands to shut them all up. I probably spoke too loud because all of a sudden, heads turned toward our table and conversations quieted down. Not again.

Simone grinned and pointed at each one who had asked a question, answering them. "Yes, no, yes, and yes."

"What? Simone!" I tugged at her arm. "What are you saying?"

She gave me a wide-eyed innocent look that I knew was the furthest from the truth. "Nothing. I'm just confirming that he was the guy at the soccer game."

I looked at my teammates. "You weren't all there. Why do you know who was at the game?"

Denise tilted her head and gave me a goofy look. "Geri, we all have InstaG. Didn't you see Simone's post?"

Simone giggled. "Sorry, Geri. I tried to crop you guys out of the background, but well, you guys looked so cute."

Why didn't I see that?

Denise pulled her phone out of her pocket and scrolled down to find the photo Simone had posted. She handed it to me and when I looked at it, I was transported back to that late afternoon at the soccer stadium. Simone and Helena were front and center, smiling, one arm around the other, and Bas and I were in the background. I was frowning at him and he was grinning at me. What were we talking about? I did remember that he was being all charming to my friends and I couldn't understand what was going on. Things were different now of course.

"Look at her face! I was right!" My head snapped up when I heard Simone's victorious cry.

"Right about what?" I slid the phone back to Denise who glanced at the photo again.

"Did you read the comments?" She chuckled. Denise held her phone up close to her face and recited, "'Who is that hottie smiling at Geri?' 'I know him! That's my buddy Bas Mercado. We do aikido together.' 'Someone hasn't been sharing.'"

I folded my arms on the tabletop and dropped my head into them. "Why can't people just leave me alone? He's just a friend, tutoring me."

"Last I heard, you hated him." Simone's finger poked my waist.

I peeked up at her. "Yeah, but..."

A chorus of whoops echoed all around me.

"You were right, Sim!"

"Geri has a boyfriend!"

I kept my face down. This was what happened when you disappeared from the team for a few weeks. Geez.

"I do not have a boyfriend!" But no one was listening to me. Then, a hush blanketed our table and I felt a tap on my head. I lifted it to see Ms. Mirasol standing behind me. I jumped to my feet. Oh no, was this going to be a replay of the last test results? This one had no bearing, though. It wasn't like the results were urgent.

"Ms. Lazaro, may I see you for a moment?"

I glanced at Simone who looked just as apprehensive as I felt. "Ms. Lazaro," she mouthed giving me a thumbs up under the table where Ms. Mirasol couldn't see. I crossed my fingers then followed our math teacher out the noisy, smelly cafeteria. I thought we were just going to stand in the muggy weather, sticky and hot because it had just rained a few minutes ago. But she led me down the corridor to the faculty room.

When we entered, we were greeted by a cool blast of air. I sat across from her desk, keeping my head down so I didn't have to respond to the questioning looks from the other teachers.

"Geri, look at me." Her smile was unlike any I had ever seen on her face. "I had a free period after your test so I decided to check the papers." She slipped mine to me. No red marks. "You got the highest in class."

"I swear, I didn't cheat!" Don't ask me why that was the first thing that came out of my mouth.

"I know you didn't. I gave you different sets. Only about three students got the same kind of test. I'm brilliant that way. And paranoid." She pushed her purple frames higher up her nose and lifted one corner of her lips.

"Is this for real?" I didn't trust myself to touch the paper. I wanted to ask her to pinch me to make sure I wasn't dreaming.

"You think it's a fluke?" She removed her glasses and wiped them on her pale pink sweater before slipping them on again and peering at me.

"I..."

"Did you feel confident after answering it? While answering it?"

"Yes," I whispered. "I did. I knew how to solve the equations. For the first time in my life. Whenever I'm faced with a math test, I usually just wing it and hope for the best. It's been working mostly, but this was the first year it didn't."

"You aren't bad at math, Geri."

"I thought I had dyscalculia."

She laughed. "You do not have a brain disorder when it comes to numbers. I think what happened was you picked up a few bad habits along the way, or your basics weren't in place. You just needed to be straightened out so to speak. And I think the motivation to pass helped too."

I nodded.

"I did a few calculations. If you keep this up till the end of the quarter, you might just pass."

I grasped the edge of her desk. "But you said I was sure to fail if I got less than an 85 in the last test."

"Yes because when I did some permutations and predictions, that's what it looked like. But this was completely unexpected. I hadn't counted on your drive." She smiled. "Or your tutor."

"You heard them talking?" I groaned.

She laughed, her eyes twinkling behind her glasses. "Yes. Don't worry. I won't tease you. Anything that brings up those math grades is good. Congratulate him for me. And congratulations too, Ms. Lazaro. You can go back to class now."

I unfolded myself from the plastic chair and, in a daze, made my way back to my classroom. I never thought of myself as good at math, as someone who could actually get the highest score on a test. But here I was breaking misconceptions I held all my life. And you know what? It felt so good. Just as good as sinking a basket, one second to the buzzer, breaking a tie. Or maybe even better.

# Chapter 13

I waited outside the dojo for Bas to finish. I had never seen him and his classmates in action before. There was a lot of bowing, slow attacking movements with arms slicing downward and opponents grabbing hold of hands and arms, twisting, pulling the attacker to the floor, flipping him in the air as his legs flew. I actually liked that. And I liked how their teacher's wide black pants looked like an unfurled fan as he demonstrated a move. I was mesmerized by it all, enjoying how Bas towered over everyone else, but when a smaller opponent squared off against him, they were able to make him twist and turn as if he weighed next to nothing.

What amazed me, though, was how calm they all seemed. And Bas's story about how aikido was the answer to his anger issues made more sense. I marveled at the mastery required over their bodies, the fluidity of the movements when done right, and the look of concentration on one particular boy's face. I felt a little ache in my chest just watching him, knowing he couldn't see me, knowing I didn't have to put on a façade and act all tough. I couldn't tear my eyes away from the class, from him.

Before I knew it, they were bowing to what looked like an ancient photo of a Japanese man, and the class was over. I didn't want Bas's classmates to see me standing outside, observing them through the glass window, so when they began to exit, I walked a few steps away, hovering near the admin office.

When I first rushed to the building, hitching a ride from Simone after class and begging her to drop me at the ballet studio slash dojo, I didn't think I'd have to deal with other people. The only thing on my mind was my burning need to tell Bas about my grade and what Ms. Mirasol had said, to rejoice with someone who worked just as hard as I did on this seemingly impossible feat.

After it seemed like the last person had left the dojo, I spotted Bas's burly frame emerge from the wooden door, his backpack slung over one shoulder. I ran up to him and skidded to a stop before I could slam into his back. He turned around. I saw the light in his eyes when they landed on me, then I watched his smile catch up. "If you're here, then that means good news."

"Yes!" I jumped up, throwing both arms in the air. Before I could land on my feet, Bas wrapped his arms around my waist and spun me around. I held on to his shoulders, laughing, my head thrown back, and squealing when he wouldn't stop.

When he finally put me down, his arms were still around my waist. "You're awesome, Geri."

I continued to grin up at him, my hands pulling him closer so I could hug him. I was about to move my head to the right when I noticed his smile fade and his expression soften. His eyes seemed to be searching mine for something, I wasn't sure what. I guess you could say I was doing the same thing because I couldn't look away. He bent his head forward, and closed the gap between us.

It didn't register. All rational thought must have dissolved or turned to mush when he whirled me around. All I knew was his lips were on mine. Soft, questioning, tentative lips. As if asking for permission. My eyes closed on their own and I tightened my grip on his shoulders, pulling him closer, answering the question. Yes. Yes. Wait. No. No! This was not supposed to be happening. This was not part of the plan.

My hands moved to his chest and I pushed him away. Not too hard. Just enough to break us apart. Just enough to see a flash of hurt cross his face before he stepped back and waited for me to gather my thoughts or blurt out why I had stopped such a beautiful, beautiful thing.

"I'm sorry, Bas, I can't."

"What's wrong, Geri? I thought..."

Something snapped inside me. "You can't just do that! Why did you do that?"

"Why did I kiss you?" He sounded bewildered. I felt myself sinking into a deep panic and the only way out was to get angry. Anger, I knew. Anger, I was comfortable with. Anger was my old friend.

"Yes." My voice stumbled over the word.

"I thought we liked each other."

"Who says I like you?" I knew it was a mistake when I said it, and it was the furthest from the truth, but I couldn't take it back. I needed this, whatever it was, to stop.

His face hardened and his expression closed off. "It's fine if you don't want to kiss me, but I didn't know you didn't even want to be my friend."

"Yeah, you're right. I don't."

"Then it's a good thing I found out now before I make an even bigger fool of myself. I thought there was something special between us. But it's not the first time I've been wrong." He pulled his backpack off the floor where he had dropped it a few seconds ago and strode off.

I didn't know how long I stood there, breathing hard, the ache in my chest close to suffocating me. What did I just do? What did I just throw away? I was just kissed by the sweetest guy I knew. Yes, I know I had just met him, but he was right. There was something special about him, about both of us— together. Whether it was because we both had issues with our fathers or because we spent all that time together working on my algebra, I couldn't pretend it didn't exist. The way I so callously did with him. Why was I dead set on killing it? Was I just so screwed up there was no way I could ever be happy?

I sank to the floor and buried my head in my arms, replaying what had happened in my head over and over. I didn't know how long I stayed like that till my cell phone rang.

"Mom?"

"Where are you, Geri?"

"At the studio. Please come and get me." She probably heard the pain in my voice because she didn't press me any further.

"I'll be there soon. Sit tight."

Like there was anything else to do.

# Chapter 14

I don't usually tell my mom stuff. I keep my anger under a tight lid inside my chest. My feelings seep out every once in a while, sometimes more often than I would like, but she can never get me to fully confide in her. When Dad left, it was easier to pretend things were back to the way they were before. To pretend I didn't see her cry in bed at night, to pretend I was okay, that we were okay. To not talk about it. And though it was hard in the beginning, it got easier. After distracting myself with a movie, a basketball game, or a ballet class, it was easier to push the emotions down. To secure them with a chain and throw away the key. Mom knew this, because although she would try to pry, she never took it too far.

So I sat in the passenger seat of her old, beat-up car, my face turned toward the window, my eyes not seeing anything whizzing by outside. I thought we were going to ride home in silence, but when she made a turn that didn't lead back to the house, that enmeshed us in bumper-to-bumper traffic, I whirled around to face her. "Where are we going? You should have turned right, Mom!"

"I normally wouldn't choose to be surrounded by unmoving cars, but this is the only way you're going to talk to me without running off." She put the car in neutral and turned to me. "Tell me what's happening, Geri. I'm not taking us home until you do."

When you're used to building a thick layer of granite around your feelings, it isn't easy to chip away at it to reveal the soft, vulnerable rawness underneath. But the past few weeks seem to have done just that. Finding out my dad didn't want me made me face past hurts I had worked so hard on pushing back, back into the darkest corners of myself. And having someone there to listen, to understand, to share what he had also gone through and how he had learned to overcome his own demons...

"Is this about the algebra test? That was today, right?"

I blinked up at my mom. For a few seconds, she had faded away and all I could see was the hurt splashed all over Bas's face. The anxiety, guilt, and shame coated my insides like oil, clinging with a tenacity my deep breaths couldn't displace.

I swallowed hard. "Well, sort of." My voice was small, but before I could turn away, my mom put her hand on my arm and squeezed. She put the car in first gear and inched forward before stopping and facing me once more. I forced a smile on my face. "I got the highest grade in class. Can you believe it?"

She gasped, surprise and delight coloring her features. "Geri, that's wonderful! We were just praying you'd pass."

"Yeah." I sighed. My heart felt like an anvil around my neck, making my shoulders droop. "And Ms. Mirasol said if I continue scoring this high for the rest of the quarter, there's a big chance I can pass it." I took a deep breath. "But I don't think that's going to happen anymore. I just screwed that up."

Mom didn't say anything. She moved the car a few more feet, put the car back in neutral and waited for me to continue. Surprisingly, I wanted to. I was so confused, I was so full of pent-up emotion, I had to make sense of it all.

"Bas kissed me."

I glanced at her and saw her bite her lip, as if trying to keep a smile from stealing over her face. "But?"

"I pushed him away and told him I didn't like him." I closed my eyes.

"Geri."

"But I do like him, Mom." That was it. I felt the tears choking me because I didn't want to give in to them.

"Then why…"

"I don't want to like him. I don't want to like anyone."

I couldn't fight the tears. When I reached up to touch my face, it was already wet. I rubbed my cheeks on my sleeves, annoyed with myself and how weak I was.

My mom didn't say anything. Traffic eased up and she was focused on taking us somewhere. When she pulled up outside our house, I was about to unbuckle my seatbelt and run out but she took my hands, pulling me to face her.

"Geri, are you afraid of getting hurt? Of falling in love?"

"Of course I'm afraid, Mom! Why aren't you?" The words came from inside that rawness, that vulnerability I had piled with what I thought was granite throughout the years. Apparently, I had just used some flimsy material that crumbled when someone applied the slightest pressure.

She pulled me into her arms and held me tight. My body trembled as I tried to take a breath. Or maybe that was because I was crying so much.

"My baby, I'm so sorry," she kept saying over and over. I didn't understand why. It wasn't her fault. When she let go, her eyes were red too. "Of course I'm scared. When you become a mom, that's the first thing you're branded with. Fear. Fear that you aren't good enough, fear that your happiness will be taken away, fear that your daughter will grow up to hate you, fear that she will turn out just like you."

I didn't understand.

"When I found out I was pregnant with you, I made a promise to myself that I was going to be strong. That I was going to turn my life around and make it work for you. But I was challenged at every turn. And when your dad left, I didn't know how I was going to hold it together for us. For you."

"But you did, Mom."

"I did what I could. When Matt first entered the picture, I pushed him away too. I pushed and pushed till I thought he was never going to come back. I mean, come on, why would he want me, I'm ten years older than him, I have a teenage daughter who hates him, and I couldn't give him the time and love he deserved."

"But like a leech, he just hung on." I grinned.

She laughed. This was not a conversation we had ever had, or one that we could have had if Matt and I hadn't talked and I hadn't apologized. "Yes, he did. But I also realized that I had to decide what I wanted to do with my life. The entire time, I was just reacting to things, trying to pick up after my mistakes, trying to sweep up the messes. Taking Matt into our lives was a big risk. I knew you were going to make life difficult and I didn't blame you for that, but I prayed you wouldn't. But for the first time, I told myself I needed to do this for me. You don't know how happy I am that you guys talked."

"Bas's fault."

"But this isn't. He's not the reason you're afraid." The pain was back in her eyes and that was when it hit me.

"No. I'm afraid he's just going to hurt me the way..."

"The way your father did."

I gulped. I've never said it out loud. I've never acknowledged that the reason I hated guys and wanted to keep them all away was because of him.

I was doomed. It was that simple.

"But this is what I had to learn, Geri." I blinked. Mom was talking again. I had almost forgotten she was there. "Not all guys are like your dad. Not all guys are going to hurt you the way he hurt you. But you'll never know that if you don't give them a chance."

Yeah, but how was I going to fix this now? I just told Bas that I didn't like him. Like a hateful, ungrateful little brat.

"I wasn't going to bring this up because I was angry when he proposed this out of the blue a few days ago. Because I didn't think he deserved this. But with everything you've told me..." My mom pressed her lips together, something she did when she was anxious about something.

"What are you talking about, Mom?"

She took a deep breath and let it out in a whoosh. "Your dad wants to see you."

"What?" I crossed my arms over my chest. "No freaking way."

"He called me to apologize. He said he finally realized how selfish he was and how he needed to make amends before moving on to the next step of his life. He met someone and he wants to marry her, but he's..." She turned away from me and stared out the dirty windshield. "He's afraid he's going to make the same mistake. He thinks, he *hopes* if he fixes this part of his life, he can move on."

"What kind of nonsense is that? Fix this? Fix us?" I felt the rage build up inside my head, and if smoke could shoot out of my ears, it would be filing up the car by now. "Say sorry and then get his happily ever after? Sorry, buster, that's not how it's going to work."

My mom looked at me again. "Sweetheart, that's not what he means. He wants to become part of our lives again. Well, your life. He and I know our story is completely different now." She lifted her lips in a soft smile. "If what he feels for this girl is the same thing I feel for Matt, then I am really happy for him. Your dad and I just weren't meant to be or maybe we weren't ready to become parents yet. And I've mourned our relationship. I've moved on. Maybe it's time for all of us to heal and get past this. What do you say?"

This issue with my dad was like an open sore that refused to scab because no matter how many times the blood would clot, something would scratch it, scraping off the dried fluid, exposing a fresh wound all over again. I grit my teeth and shook my head. "No, Mom. He can rot in you know where for all I care."

She sighed. "You might still change your mind."

"I won't." With that, I yanked on the door handle and leapt out of the car, hoping I could leave all the pain behind when I slammed the door.

# Chapter 15

"I can't believe you're finally going to see him again after all this time. What are you going to talk about?" Helena pulled out two dresses from my crammed closet and held them up against her lithe body.

Simone, who was sprawled on the floor with her feet up on my bed, stuck out her tongue. "I don't think she needs to make an effort for the man who abandoned her, Hel."

Helena frowned at Simone, returned the dresses and pulled out another one. It was dark blue, sleeveless, and fell to my knees. The length worked because it didn't show too much leg. My dad might appreciate it if I looked conservative. But then again, who cared what he thought?

Mom was right. I changed my mind after stumbling into my room and turning to face my empty wall, now devoid of Michael Jordan. I was about to talk to him the way I usually did, out of habit. I was ready to rant to him about my dad being so presumptuous and arrogant, thinking just because his life was working out that he could all of a sudden include me in it. But Michael was gone. Just like my dad. I stood there staring at the wall, a flood of feelings drowning my senses. Afraid I was going to burst, I ran out of my room, down the stairs, and almost collided with my mom who was just entering the front door. Out of breath, I told her I was willing to see him. Just once. Just to get it over with.

So now my friends were helping me get ready to have

lunch with him. "I'll wear that one." I jumped up from the bed and started wriggling out of the shorts and tee I'd slept in.

Helena laid the dress on my messy sheets and began smoothening it out. "You know, Sim, no matter how much of a you-know-what Geri's dad is, he's still her flesh and blood."

"Well, I don't think she should push through with this." Simone lifted her arms and cradled her head in her hands. "What does Bas think?"

Helena shot me a look. I told her about what happened but I made her swear not to tell anyone. I knew Simone was going to torture me about it. But the sound of his name made my heart hurt.

"What happened, Ger?" Simone pushed herself up on her elbows and squinted at me as if I were a new play Coach wanted to try and she was learning it for the first time.

Helena sighed. "Bas kissed her."

"What?"

"Helena!"

"How you could expect me to keep this a secret is beyond me, Geri!" She sounded like Teacher Justine reprimanding me for not keeping my chin up or my leg straight.

"Geri Lazaro, why didn't you tell me about this?" Simone was on her feet, her hands on her hips.

I glowered at them both. "Because of this! Exactly this! I thought Helena was going to be quiet about it and not get mad at me, but I guess I was wrong." I grabbed the dress from the bed and yanked it over my head.

When I finally pulled it over my eyes, Simone was standing in front of me, her eyes shining with what could only be excitement. "How was it?"

I sank back down on the bed and started brushing my hair, which was still frustratingly short. "It was..."

"It was beautiful!" Helena squealed, her hands on Simone's arm. They started jumping up and down. "That was the word she used, can you believe it?"

"Oh, Geri, I knew it! I just knew it!" Simone threw her arms around me. I shoved her away and continued brushing my hair. What dorks. She frowned at me. "Okay, I'm guessing from your level of excitement that this story does not end well. Oh no, Geri, did you slap him or something? Please tell me you didn't."

"She didn't, but she told him she didn't like him," Helena muttered.

"What? That's a lie!"

I threw the brush down on the bed. "Can you two stop talking about me like I'm not here?"

"When did this happen? How long have you allowed him to think you don't like him?" Simone planted her feet in front of me.

"Too long." Helena frowned.

I stared at her with my mouth wide open. "I just told you about this yesterday! This happened like two days ago!"

"And in those two days, you never tried to get in touch with Bas to apologize? To let him know that you didn't mean what you said?" Simone bent down and put her hands on my cheeks, her eyes boring into mine.

I shook my head. "I tried. I composed about a dozen text messages but I kept erasing them. None of them sounded right. They all came out stupid."

"I don't think it matters what you say as long as you make the effort, Geri." Helena squeezed my shoulder.

Before I could reply, my mom pushed my bedroom door open and stuck her head through the gap. "Are you ready, Geri? Let's go."

I straightened up and followed my mom out the door, Helena and Simone right behind me. I threw my arms around both of them before getting into my mom's car. "Wish me luck." I felt my heart hammering against my chest and my tummy swish acid around as if a tsunami were wreaking havoc inside it.

"Just remember." Helena took both my hands. "Protect your heart."

I nodded, but I realized I had no idea how to do that. So far, I was doing a pretty bad job.

Mom wanted to meet in a restaurant so we'd be on neutral ground. She didn't think my dad would feel comfortable in our house, where he might become consumed by guilt, or where he would completely feel like an outsider in a place he used to call home. And she was right in thinking I didn't want to visit his place.

Mom picked a Japanese noodle house. If you asked me, she couldn't have chosen a messier place to eat. She was an expert at slurping her noodles while I struggled. No matter how carefully I ate, I always managed to get soup on my face and clothes. But that wasn't surprising. I wasn't exactly the most graceful teenager when I wasn't dancing.

As we stepped into the cozy interiors, with its low ceiling and wooden tables and benches, I was glad my mom didn't choose a fancy place. That would have been more stressful. Maybe she also didn't want to put extra pressure on all of us. Even if I didn't really want to be here, I was anxious about seeing my dad again after all this time. I had no idea what to expect.

He was already there, sitting alone at a table in the corner. He was bent over his phone, his shoulders tense, his brow furrowed. He was smaller than I remembered. Thinner, and definitely older. His hair, which used to be wavy and black, was now streaked with gray. His thick eyebrows, the same shape as mine, the eyebrows Mom kept asking me to wax or thread, were also peppered with short white strands. I didn't realize I was staring till Mom squeezed my arm, jolting me into action.

"Hi, Dad."

His eyes flew up, dark, round, with lines on the sides. Before his face creased into a smile, I saw the apprehension on his face. It probably mirrored my own unsmiling one.

"Geri. Anna." He got up and walked awkwardly around the rectangular wooden table to stand before us.

His shoulders were still broad and he was still several inches taller than me, but maybe the weirdness of the situation had shrunk him somehow. The aura surrounding him felt much smaller than the booming charm that used to accompany my dashing father wherever he went. He leaned down to press his cheek against my mom's. She smiled, her eyes softening as he came closer. It was then that I realized she wasn't lying. She had actually forgiven him. Or she was no longer angry. I didn't sense any tension coming from her. It was all him. And me.

He turned to me, taking a breath before leaning down and kissing me on the cheek. I stiffened when he came close. *Relax, Geri. Try not to make this worse than it already is.* I forced a smile and said, "Let's sit?"

My mom plopped down next to me and motioned for my dad to sit across from us. She took my hand under the table and held it. I was grateful she was there, but at the same time, I wondered what it would be like if it were just me and my dad. But then, what on earth would we talk about?

We passed a few minutes talking about what to order, what kind of ramen we liked, and Dad tried to make small talk by asking where else Mom and I liked to eat. I almost said that

Matt insisted on taking us out to fancy restaurants to celebrate one thing or another, but I didn't think it would come out right. And weirdly enough, I felt disloyal to Matt by even thinking it. It was unsettling because I got so used to thinking angry thoughts about him, and now I suddenly felt like he was on my team, as opposed to the father I thought would always be on my side.

When Mom excused herself to go to the bathroom, I shot her a panicked look, which she ignored. Great. Now what? We were still waiting for our food, so it wasn't like I could pretend I was focusing on something else.

"So, your mom says you still play ball?"

"I used to." I didn't want to talk to him about this.

"But you're on the team, right?" He sounded confused.

"Yes."

"Benched?"

I looked up into his eyes, catching a glimpse of the challenge I used to see in them when I was a kid, when he taught me how to play basketball.

"Sort of. I need to bring up my algebra grades first then I can play again," I mumbled, tearing the paper napkin next to me into tiny pieces.

"You can't neglect your studies for sports, Geri. No matter how good you are."

My mouth fell open and I glared at him. "You have no right to tell me what to do."

He leaned back as if I'd slapped him. Which, I guess, I did with my words. But why the hell did he think he could tell me what to do when he had made the choice to leave? To have nothing to do with me?

"I'm still your father, Geri." His voice was soft, but I didn't care how much pain I saw behind those eyes, eyes that looked so much like mine.

"I don't think you can call yourself my father after disappearing from my life and not wanting to come back."

"Geri." It was my mom. Her voice was low, controlled, but I could hear the warning laced through those two syllables.

"I'm sorry," I mumbled. "Maybe this was a mistake. Maybe I wasn't ready to see you."

My mom sat down and put her hands on the table. "Let's start again okay? John, maybe you can tell us about your work?"

I appreciated her trying to take control, trying to diffuse the tension. And it worked. We chatted about his job. He now worked for a trading company, and he met his girlfriend Janna on a blind date when his officemates forced him to go on one. He said he never expected to fall for her. But he did. He was careful about praising his new woman. Maybe afraid of hurting Mom? Or hurting me? That was when I felt I had to let him know that we were fine without him. "Matt's a regular fixture in the house. Yaya Agnes loves him more than she loves any of us."

Mom snorted.

"It's true!" Well, except maybe for Bas. He and Matt were in competition for who Yaya Agnes loved to feed the most.

I don't know if my dad got the hint, but my parents started reminiscing and talking about Yaya Agnes after what I said. I found it weird but at the same time, I sort of liked how they seemed to be friends. Not angry at each other, not like me.

After we had eaten the ramen I could hardly taste because of how self-conscious and annoyed I was, and before Dad could ask if we could go somewhere else for dessert, Mom said, "Geri has to study, John. We need to go. But thank you for lunch. This...this was nice." Nice? I had a better word for it.

"Maybe we can do it again?" I knew he was looking at me but I had my phone out and was scrolling through whatever I could find just to avoid scheduling another awkward meeting with him.

Mom answered for me, thankfully. "Just text me, John."

"Can I message you too, Geri?"

I had to hand it to him. He wasn't allowing one unfortunate lunch to ruin his life goals. "Mom can send you my number."

When he leaned down to kiss my cheek, I shoved my phone into my tote and leaned forward. "Bye, Dad," I mumbled, knowing this was not going to be the last time I saw him. And I didn't know how to feel about that.

~~~

When we got home, I tore off my dress and pulled on an old basketball jersey and shorts. I had to shoot some hoops. I couldn't study like this. My mind was racing and so was my heart. It was just too much to take and if I was going to sit down and flip open an algebra book, I was going to implode.

Mom was on the couch, her laptop in front of her. She looked up, took in my outfit, and sighed. "Geri."

"Just a few hoops, Mom. I'll be back soon."

"Fine. Then I want you to study."

I kissed her on the cheek and ran out, jogging all the way to our village park a few blocks away. Despite it being early afternoon, the air was cool, the sky covered in light gray clouds. It had been drizzling all day, but I welcomed the weather. It beat the thick humidity or the blazing Manila sun.

I didn't waste any time. Glad no one else was on the court, I began practicing my free throws. One. Swish. Two. Swish. Three. Swish. See that, Dad? I may be benched but I can still sink 'em. I imagined he was playing against me, the way he did when I was a kid. Keeping pace with me as I dribbled the ball, my body bent, my eyes on my target. He used to tell me to be aware of his movements, not to ignore my opponent who was studying my moves too. It was like a dance, but one we didn't choreograph. A dance that played off each other. I imagined him reaching up to block my shot so I faked left, spun, and ran right up to the basket. Beat that, Dad.

"Nice shot. But it's never as fun when you're playing alone."

I grabbed the ball and turned around. Matt. He had a water jug in his hands.

"Hey. Did Mom send you with that?"

"Yeah." He was in sneakers and jeans, but when he put the jug down, I threw him the ball. He caught it and ran past me to do an easy layup. I scooped up the ball, darted out to the three-point line and jumped. Bounced off the rim. Matt grabbed the ball and made another clean shot. After doing this a few times, he asked, "How did it go?"

"Meeting my dad?" I passed the ball to him. He took the shot.

"Yeah. Your mom just shrugged when I asked her." He threw me a chest pass.

I laughed, catching the ball. "Now that I'm out of there, I can say it wasn't as bad as it could have been." I dropped the ball and walked over to the jug of water to take a drink. After wiping my mouth with the back of my hand, I handed it to him.

"Must have been hell for him though." He took a swig.

"Whose side are you on?" But I wasn't mad. Surprisingly, I was amused.

"I can't help but feel for him because he's the guy." He shrugged, looking sheepish. "That could very well have been me."

"Because of the weakness of your gender?" I raised an eyebrow.

It was his turn to laugh. "Maybe. I was just wondering what I would do if I were in his place."

"I didn't get to ask him why he left." I picked up the ball again and ran for the basket. I wasn't tall enough for a dunk so I settled for a layup. "Maybe I don't want to know."

"Or maybe now's not the time yet." He looked at me as if debating whether to tell me something or not. "Your mom said he felt suffocated and needed to find himself. That's what he told her."

I was about to shrug it off the way I always did. Pretend it didn't matter to me. Pretend the thought didn't feel like searing acid tearing a hole through my brain. But one look at Matt's concerned eyes and I nodded. "Yeah, I know. Maybe I'll understand when I'm older."

"Or maybe you don't need to understand, but just accept that's how things are? Makes it simpler that way sometimes."

Wise words. Then I smirked. "Now I know the secret of how you deal with me and my mom."

Matt laughed.

I was about to pivot on my heel and attempt another shot when he called out, "Geri, I wanted to ask for your help with something."

I brought the ball down and balanced it on my hip. "Sure, what is it?"

He took a few steps closer and stopped when he was right in front of me. He dug into his pocket and pulled out something tiny, something I couldn't see properly till he held it out to me. I gasped, dropping the ball, my hands flying to my mouth. It was a sparkly diamond embedded in a ring of white gold. "Oh, wow." I breathed. "You're going to make Mom so happy."

I felt the tears prick my eyes. If there was anyone who deserved to be happy, it was my mom. And Matt. I blinked the tears away and smiled at him.

"I was hoping you'd say something like that." He grinned, putting it back in his pocket.

"Not something like, 'are you out of your mind?'" I teased.

He laughed. "I would have died if you said that." Then his face turned serious again. "I know we can be a family, Geri. I don't want to replace your dad, but I want to be part of your life too. And I'm going to need help. I have no idea how to propose."

"I have some ideas." I held out my hand for him to shake. "Welcome to the family, Matt."

He shook my hand, then pulled me into an embrace. I hugged him back, thinking Bas would be so proud of me. If only we were still talking.

# Chapter 16

"What are you doing?"

I looked up as my mom entered my room. I was on the floor, my math books open in front of me, crumpled balls of paper littered all around, some next to my purple mesh trash can. Yeah, I can sink my free throws but not all my paper tosses. Especially when I'm distracted.

"I'm trying to study." I spread my hands above my notebooks.

She frowned. "I heard a few thumps and weird noises so I rushed here to find out if you were still alive."

She bent down and started picking up the balls of paper. She tossed a few into the trash can, but before throwing the last one in, she smoothed it out and started scanning it. I scrambled to my feet and tried to snatch it from her but she was quick. She darted away, still trying to read what I had written.

"These aren't algebra equations, Geri." She jumped on my bed and scurried to the corner. As if I couldn't reach her there. I pounced on her and grabbed the paper, ripping it in two.

"Mom! You're not supposed to read that!" I tried to snatch the other piece from her, but she stuffed it into her mouth.

I burst out laughing.

She spat it out and shoved me off the bed. "Why are you keeping secrets from me, Geri Lazaro?"

I looked up at her from where I landed on the floor. "I'm a teenager, Mom. That's what we do."

"Well, I read most of it. Looks like you're trying to compose an apology to someone." She aimed for the trash can and in went the damp piece of paper. Eww. My mom can be so gross sometimes.

I groaned. "Yeah but it's not enough."

"So you've changed your mind? About Bas? About giving him a chance?"

My heart twisted in symmetry with my gut, a perfect pas de deux. "Something happened this afternoon that changed my mind."

"Meeting with your dad? How on earth could that disaster have changed your mind? I would have thought you'd be burying your head under your pillows and telling me you never want to see another boy for as long as you live."

"That's why I needed to go shoot some hoops after." I pressed my lips against each other. "But no, Dad has nothing to do with this. And well, after that thing happened, it hit me that you were right."

Mom studied me, as if the cogs in her brain were spinning. I wondered if she was going to push and ask what I was talking about. To my relief, she smiled. "If you wanted to tell me what it was, you would have. But I think I can guess—"

"No you can't."

She laughed. "Anyway. I'm glad."

Mom started to get up and I tugged on the fabric of her cotton pants. "Where are you going? Aren't you going to help me out with this?"

She shook her head. "This is something you have to come up with on your own. You can do it, Geri."

"Thanks a lot, Mom," I muttered, putting as much sarcasm in my tone as I could so she wouldn't miss it.

"You're welcome, honey!" She winked and gave me a little wave as she closed the door.

Well, if she wasn't going to help me, I was sure Helena would. I took my phone off my nightstand and was about to send her a message when a reminder flashed on my screen.

*Aikido Demonstration, 6PM.*

What? That was today? I had completely forgotten about it. My head began to spin. Why didn't Bas say anything? What on earth was he going to do when all this time we had been practicing to perform as a pair? The guilt started seeping into my vital organs. Of course he couldn't say anything. I told him I didn't want to be his friend, that I didn't like him. How could he have called and asked me to dance with him after that? I wanted to cry, but I knew what I had to do. I had a little over an hour to get to the gym. I jumped up, grabbed my tights, skirt, and leotard from my closet and pulled them on as fast as I could.

"Mom!" I hollered, running down the stairs. She was in the kitchen discussing something with Yaya Agnes. "Can you please, please take me to Budo-kan Gym?"

"What? Why?"

"I'll explain on the way. But we need to hurry."

She grabbed her keys and was out the door before I was.

I didn't get to plan anything. I didn't get to rehearse any lines of apology. I was a ball of anxiety in a leotard and tights. I stood outside the gym's entrance, watching the people trickle in. I headed for the rickety looking registration table and asked where I could find Bas Mercado. The guy sitting at the table frowned at me, probably wondering why I looked the way I did. So before he could say anything, I blurted, "I'm here to perform with him."

His expression cleared and he motioned to a person standing behind him in a black shirt with an official looking ID. "Ron, take her backstage with the rest of the performers."

I waited for Ron to lead me inside, but he was too busy taking in my outfit and giving me a puzzled look. The way Registration guy did. "Are you sure you're in the right place?" Ron cocked his head to the side.

"Yes. Can you just take me to Bas?"

He nodded and motioned for me to follow him in. He mentioned something I didn't hear to the guy at the door. When we stepped through, the first thing I noticed was the huge red mat in the middle. There were no chairs, and people had taken their places on the floor. "I thought there was going to be a stage."

"Have you ever been to an aikido demonstration before?" Ron still looked a bit confused. I guess I should have come in regular clothes but I didn't want to waste any time dressing up when I got there. Plus, I had to convince Bas that he still wanted to dance with me. Who knew how long that would take?

I shook my head. "There's a first time for everything. No wonder he didn't want me to do this en pointe."

"En what?"

"Nothing. Where's Bas?" I didn't want to sound impatient, but if this Ron guy was just going to stand there looking at me, I wasn't going to accomplish anything. And I already felt I was about to explode, like a boiled egg being reheated in a microwave. It's happened to me a few times, much to Yaya Agnes's frustration.

"I don't see him anywhere but I'm in charge of the line up. Do you need anything for your performance? Bas is fifth on the list. Now that you're here, I remember he told me there was a change in the program. He originally needed music but—"

I handed him my phone and showed him the screen. "Here it is. I can put in the passcode when it's time for us to go on."

His eyes lit up. "Great! Let me just hook it up."

When he jogged away to some place in the back, I looked around, hoping to find the one person I was desperate to see.

There was no air-conditioning in this gym, but the huge air coolers placed at strategic points next to electric fans cooled the entire place. Plus, the high ceiling and open windows kept it from being stuffy. There were quite a few people sitting on the floor, mostly kids my age. Probably here to support their friends. Or curious about aikido. There was also that photo of the ancient looking Japanese guy on a table that resembled an altar of sorts. I still had to ask Bas about that and why they had to keep bowing to him.

Ron was taking so long and I couldn't see Bas anywhere, so I started walking around. I noticed some people sneaking looks at me. Well, I kind of asked for it by wearing an outfit that was clearly out of place.

"Geri, what are you doing here?"

I spun around, my heart drumming out a conga rhythm in my ears. "Hi, Bas! We're performing, right?"

His face was unreadable, closed off, as if he didn't want anything to do with me. "*I am going to perform.*"

"No, we are going to perform together." I took his hand and pulled him to the side, away from the people, away from the noise.

He tugged his hand away and gestured for me to follow him around a corner where they kept standees and some equipment. It was cramped but I was glad we weren't in the middle of a crowd.

"Bas." I didn't want him to push me away before I said something—anything—to make this right between us. "I'm so sorry about what happened. I wasn't thinking, I wasn't..."

I looked at his face and saw he was listening to me, his eyes on mine. I couldn't look away and all the words flew out of my head. So I did the only other thing I could think of. I stood on my toes, put my hands on his shoulders, and pressed my lips against his. I had no idea what I was doing or whether it was a smart thing to do, but I knew it was what I wanted. And if this was how I could convey all the feelings I couldn't express properly through words, then it was the most wonderful thing of all.

His arms wrapped around my waist, pulling me closer, and a sigh escaped me. It was okay. We were going to be okay. And we were going to dance. When he lifted his head to look at me, I saw a storm of emotion in his eyes.

"Geri."

"I didn't mean what I said to you at the dojo, Bas. I need you to know that."

He tightened his arms around me, pulling me into the warmest, most comforting hug. But before he could say anything, we heard someone clearing his throat next to us. It was Ron, his face red, probably from embarrassment. But I didn't let go.

I squeezed Bas even tighter then leaned back to gaze at his face. His adorably handsome face. "There's a lot I need to tell you. But right now," I gave him a small smile, "will you dance with me?"

# Chapter 17

It had been days since we last practiced together, but it felt as if Bas and I knew exactly how to stand and which hands to grasp as we got into position right before the crowd. My heart pounded in my chest, not because I was nervous, but because of what just happened. When I decided to rush to the gym to dance with Bas, I wasn't ready to tell him what I felt and I most definitely wasn't ready to kiss him again. The same way we needed a few more practices before we were ready to face an audience. But based on how things were going over the past few days, life didn't seem to work that way. As Matt said, sometimes, you don't need to understand, you just have to accept things as they are: complicated and messy.

As his sensei said a few words about the last demonstration, I looked up at Bas, trying to keep my hands steady.

"Are you nervous?" he whispered, looking a bit tense himself.

"I'm not sure. Maybe. I've never performed with a partner before."

"What? And here I thought I chose the best ballerina in class!"

I stuck my tongue out at him. "We can do this."

"I know you can."

I closed my eyes and let his words wash over me. I knew I could too, but hearing him say them that way, full of faith and trust, took my breath away.

The sensei introduced us, saying this was Bas's idea and that he wanted to do something different to show how aikido had changed his life. My eyes flew open and I stared at him. "I didn't know that's why we're doing this."

He smiled at me, all the earlier tension gone, as if he had made peace with the performance in the few seconds I had my eyes closed. "That's why there's no one else I want to dance with but you."

The slow introductory strains of our song came on. It wasn't a classic ballet instrumental piece. It wasn't from *Camelot* either, but a song I came across recently called "Peter Pan" by Kelsea Ballerini. It was a song about heartbreak, about being a naïve, young girl who learned that the boy she loved wasn't who she thought he was. I loved the emotion, the pain. As I moved, gliding my arms above my head and in front of me, as Bas took my hand and began flipping, his legs kicking through the air, I realized why it spoke to me.

When I first played it for Bas, I liked how the words "fly away" could correspond to a grand jete and a high flip, but it hit me just then, while we were dancing, why I had taken this song as my own—as part of the soundtrack to my life. Because it might as well have been written for my father. But as Bas put his hands around my waist and lifted me in the air as if I were no lighter than a pillow, I also knew that it didn't matter if my father wasn't who I thought he was. It didn't matter if my dad had broken my heart. Because even if he had flown away, even if he had to leave us to find himself, I could forgive him. I could move on. And I could let go of the fear that all boys were going to hurt me the way he did.

As Bas rolled and flipped, I leapt and twirled. Our arms weaved in and out, around and above each other. Our hands touched, light and shy at first, then as the music rose together with the pain and longing of each word, we hung on tight as we propelled ourselves into the air. It felt like we had been dancing together forever. This weird dance that wasn't even really a dance, but a conversation. A challenge, a promise.

At first, I was trying hard to remember what the steps were, my brow knit and my lips drawn out into my practiced, plastered stage smile. But after a few beats, I decided to follow Bas's lead and allow the music and his movements to transport me into that other world, the one I disappeared to whenever I danced. My heart swelled and my feet flew across the mat because I knew he was right there with me. As if the audience had fallen away and we were making up the steps as we moved, answering each other's motions as if they were questions, saying yes. Yes to losing ourselves in an art form, yes to taking that frightening leap, yes to moving in sync with each other.

When I spun in a series of pique and chaines turns, focusing on Bas, landing in his arms, and stretching upward for the final pose as the last note of the song played, I knew we had done it. We accomplished something we thought had only been a dream. As the audience clapped, whistled, hooted, and cheered for more, I flashed him a huge smile. He tightened his grip around my waist then dropped his hand and captured mine in his as I curtseyed. I let go of his hand and lifted my arm, presenting him to the audience, encouraging him to take his own bow. When he bent his upper body, a few of the kids in the audience returned the gesture. I curtseyed again and was about to turn and run off to the side when he took my hand and pulled me to him, slinging his arm around me. I grinned up at him and we exited together as his sensei took the microphone and thanked us for what he called "a surprisingly moving performance."

As soon as we were off the mat, away from the performance area, I threw my arms around him and held him tight. "We did it!"

He hugged me back and kissed the top of my head. "Yes, we did. Thank you for not deserting me."

I pulled back and looked into his eyes, wanting to tell him everything but knowing this was not the place. "Do you need to stay for the entire show?"

He nodded and released me, taking my hand again. "If not, Sensei is going to kill me. Want to watch with me?"

I didn't know how I was going to wait till after the show before we could talk, but as I sat on the mat, my legs tucked under me, my hand wrapped in his, I felt like I could stay by his side forever.

〰〰

I heard the rain before I saw it. Bas and I ran out of the gym only to skid to a stop when we saw the downpour.

"How are we going to get to your car now?" I glanced down at my ballet shoes. "My feet will get soaked!"

"I'll carry you." Bas smirked.

"I don't think so."

"I'll find an umbrella. Maybe you can ride on my back?"

"This isn't a Korean drama, Bas."

"Get your feet wet then." He disappeared into the crowd behind us, people on their cell phones calling for their drivers or waiting for the rain to let up.

"Look what I found!" In a few seconds, he was back by my side waving a pair of high cut basketball shoes. "I forgot I brought two pairs."

I put a hand on my hip. "Okay. And?"

"You can wear these so you won't get wet."

"No way."

"Try them on. You don't need to remove your ballet shoes."

I plunged my right foot into one humongous shoe and laughed when Bas started lacing it up. "I'm going to trip in these."

"You can hang on to me."

I smiled at his earnest expression.

He lifted a battered looking umbrella and struggled with opening it.

"Are you sure that thing works?"

"I found it in the locker room. It was the only one left." He finally pushed it open and held it above our heads.

I grabbed on to his arm and put one heavy foot in front of the other. So far, his shoes weren't falling off my feet. We crossed the street in front of the gym and began making our way to the parking lot when a blast of wind upended our umbrella. Bas tried to yank it back but it wouldn't return to its original shape.

"It's broken!" I yelled.

He put a hand over my head as if to keep the rain away, and we burst out laughing at how ridiculous we looked. Me with my clown-sized feet, Bas hanging on to a useless umbrella, and the rain soaking us to the skin. He whipped off his white kimono top and draped it around my shoulders. I was about to argue that the rain was just going to make it heavier, but since I was in a thin, light pink leotard, I realized any other material was better defense against water and indecency.

His black shirt was already clinging to him, and I couldn't help reaching out to poke his tummy.

He looked down and grabbed my hand. "Stop! Are you trying to tickle me?"

"Just wanted to make sure I didn't imagine those abs." I chuckled.

"You didn't."

I rolled my eyes and started stomping forward again. He caught my arm and fell in step next to me. All of a sudden, the rain came down even harder. I yelped and ran as fast as I could in Bas's ginormous shoes under the nearest tree. It looked like an acacia with its leaves creating a canopy of sodden green over a stone bench. I sank onto the partially wet seat and lifted Bas's shoes to drain the water that had pooled inside them.

"I guess wearing my shoes didn't work." He sounded mournful.

"It was still very thoughtful of you." When I didn't get a reply, I put his shoes down and turned to face him. He had a strange look on his face. "What?"

He shook his head. "I'm just not used to this side of you."

"The side that says what she feels instead of just what she thinks?"

"I never thought the inside of your head was such a war zone."

"You didn't know what you were getting into."

"Doesn't mean I still don't want to be here." He took my clammy hand in his warm one. "I never wanted to be anywhere else, Geri, since the first time I saw you dance."

"You could have fooled me." But I felt the heat creeping up my cold cheeks and I was grateful for the dark.

"Well, I didn't want my feelings spliced open for you to trample on. You've got to admit, you would have."

I grimaced. He was right. "But not anymore!" I held his hand tighter.

"Yeah." He smiled. "You said there was a lot you wanted to tell me."

I took a deep breath and looked out at the rain coming down in sheets. It was so strong, the leaf canopy wasn't enough to protect us. But it didn't matter, we were already drenched. "I finally saw my dad. We had lunch." I glanced at him, rubbing my face against the sleeve of his kimono jacket. "It didn't go that well. You know how Helena keeps saying I'm so combative? Well, I brought my A game." I let out a short laugh. "But my mom stopped me from ruining the meal further. It was awkward, but my dad seems to think we're seeing each other again."

"It's going to get better."

I smiled at him. Glad he was speaking from experience and not just spouting platitudes to reassure me. "Yeah but you see, my dad had nothing to do with this realization of mine. Or maybe he has everything to do with it. If he hadn't left my mom, she never would have fallen in love with Matt." I swallowed. "I knew I was wrong about him, but I didn't know how wrong." I turned to Bas and clutched both his hands, not minding the rain spilling down my face. "He wants to marry my mom, Bas. We're going to be a family."

He pulled me to him, against his chest. "That's wonderful, Geri."

"It made me realize that there's hope."

"I already told you that," he murmured against my head.

"Yeah but you know me."

"I do."

I heard the laughter rumbling in his chest and closed my eyes. "Bas, will you plan his proposal with me?"

He leaned back and smiled down at me. "Only if you allow me a little proposal of my own."

I frowned at him. "What?"

"I don't want things to be unclear. The way you think, I'm pretty sure I'll be in the middle of another battle with you tomorrow."

"Bas!"

He cupped my cheeks with his large hands and said, "Geri Lazaro, based on the past few weeks, I know it's going to be one helluva ride, but I'm willing to hang on for as long as you'll have me. Will you be my girlfriend?"

I opened my mouth but no words came out. Was he always going to reduce me to silence every time something significant happened? My eyes dropped to his lips, his soft, soft lips, and I smiled. Well, if that was how it was going to be, I didn't have a problem with it. I reached up and tugged his neck down so his mouth was aligned with mine and I kissed him again and again and again.

"I take that as a yes?" He was as breathless as I was.

I rubbed my face against his and laughed softly. "Yes, Bas. Yes. Yes. Yes."

# Chapter 18

I pulled down on the rusty switch, flooding the stage with different colored lights. I bit my lip to keep the grin from stealing over my face. We weren't in the clear yet. I turned to Helena whose big, round eyes reflected back the anxiety in mine. Simone tapped both our shoulders, adjusting her professional-looking headset.

"We have a few more minutes before she shows up. Are you two ready?" she asked.

I glanced at Helena and nodded. "Yes."

Simone turned her face away from us, listening to something on her headphones. She brought a hand up to the microphone attached underneath her chin and barked, "Yes. Okay. We're ready. Cue music."

I looked up into the control booth and could make out a burly figure moving around, most likely following Simone's instructions. She waved us forward and Helena and I padded out onstage. Well, I padded and Helena floated. We were dressed in last year's recital costumes, an emerald green bodice with gold embroidery stitched down the front and a stiff tutu that flared out from our hips. I had on my favorite pointe shoes and a flower in my hair for good luck.

I held my breath as I looked out at the empty auditorium, dark and deep, filled with promise. A few days ago, we asked

Teacher Justine if we could borrow the hall where we held our annual recital. When we told her what our plans were, she said yes right away. Since we were going to do it in the early afternoon, no one was going to use it to practice anyway.

As the opening strains of the familiar melody began to play, flowing into each corner of the theater, Helena and I took our positions. The triangle of light beneath the door directly in front of the stage lengthened and widened as it was pushed open. That was our cue.

Helena and I began our combinations, leaping, hopping, and twirling around each other. A dance we choreographed a few days ago to Alanis Morissette's "Head Over Feet," the song my mom said perfectly captured what her brain couldn't articulate but her heart wanted to proclaim from the mountaintops. Yes, ladies and gentlemen, my sappy mother. But when I listened to the words and as we came up with the fun, light steps, I knew she was right. Matt did deserve this song. He did win her over and she did fall for him head over feet.

As they came nearer, my mom clasped her hands together and beamed. She took a seat front and center, watching us. Matt had a huge grin on his face too. I just hoped he had the ring ready or else this entire production would be wasted. Helena and I ran down the short stairs on both sides of the stage and took her hands. We led her up as Simone brought out a golden chair with plush purple upholstery—part of the recital set Teacher Justine allowed us to borrow. We made her sit in it, ignoring her questioning look. Bas dimmed the lights and Matt walked behind us, his hands in his pockets. I caught his nervous look and flashed him what I hoped was a reassuring smile.

Helena and I disappeared into the wings, trying to eavesdrop, but we couldn't hear whatever Matt was saying. All we could see was he was on his knees in front of my mom whose hands were covering her mouth as she stared at him. As he dug into his pocket for the ring, I grabbed Helena's shoulders and I felt someone else grasp my arms from behind. It was Simone. We were all holding our breath, waiting, our eyes fixed on what was happening on stage. When my mom jumped up and threw her arms around Matt and the ring clattered to the floor, I swooped in and grabbed it before it disappeared. I ran up to them and held it out, my tears making it hard for me to breathe.

My mom let go of Matt and threw her arms around me. "Thank you, Geri. I didn't expect this at all. None of it."

I hugged her back as tight as I could. But I couldn't help mumbling, "Mom, if you aren't going to put this ring on, I'm going to keep it and pawn it so I can finally buy myself a new cell phone."

She laughed, and wiping tears from her eyes, held out her left hand. I looked down at the ring in my fingers and turned to Matt, who stood there, his eyes shining too. "I think this is your job."

He smiled at me and took the ring. As he slid it on her fourth finger, I felt my breath catch. This was it. He did it. Then he looked up at me and mouthed, "We did it. Thank you."

Simone, Helena, and Bas were suddenly next to me, congratulating Matt and my mom. Tears streamed down Helena's face and Bas's eyes looked suspiciously teary. I stood next to him and slipped my hand in his. "Thank you," I whispered.

"Anytime, Geri." He put his arm around me as Helena and Simone recounted what we had done to prepare for the proposal.

"But you do know the next step is planning the wedding. You need to help me with that too." I smirked as Bas's eyes widened in panic.

"I didn't sign up to plan a wedding! I heard those are stressful enough to kill you."

I put my hands on my waist and raised an eyebrow. "I do recall someone telling me he knew it was going to be a helluva ride, but he wanted to be with me through it all."

He made a face. "Fine, fine." Then leaned down and kissed my nose.

"Hey, we're all still here!" Simone was standing right in front of us, her eyes narrowed.

"Just making sure Bas knows what he's in for over the next few months."

"More kissing?" Simone pretended to stick a finger down her throat while retching.

"Oh, we're going to make sure there's a lot of that during the wedding!" Helena clapped her hands and giggled.

"I think you should leave the planning to me." I grimaced.

"Or maybe me. I am the bride, you know." My mom put her arm around me and smiled at us. "Come on, let's go get some ice cream. My treat."

"Go ahead, I'll just make sure everything is turned off in the control booth." Bas jogged off the stage.

As they walked out the auditorium, I waited for Bas by the door. When he came running to me, he offered me his hand. I took it and smiled. "So are you ready? Because from here on, it's just going to get crazier."

He looked out at the empty auditorium, then back at me. His eyes twinkled in the darkness. "I meant what I said, Geri. As long as you'll have me."

"That can be for a very long time. I just realized how much fun it is to have you around." I grinned. His lips touched mine for a brief second, then he pushed open the heavy door.

"Yeah? So what are you standing around here for? Bring it on, Geri Lazaro!"

I squeezed his hand. "You're on, Bas Mercado."

As we ran out laughing into the bright Manila sunshine to get some ice cream with my favorite people in the world, I didn't think my heart could get any fuller than it already was.

● ● ●

# Not Quite The End Yet

● ● ●

When I got home that night, after spending the rest of the afternoon gorging on ice cream and French fries, I pushed open the door of my room and stood before the blank wall by my bed. I turned to the *balikbayan* box in the corner, the one I still couldn't bring myself to throw away, and pulled out the rolled up poster of Michael Jordan. I dropped it on my bed, took some sticky tac from my desk, and began pushing the little balls I had formed with my fingers into the wall, using the dust outline as my guide. I unrolled the poster and pressed its corners against the tiny mounds of clay.

I plopped down on my bed and faced Michael. "Welcome back, buddy. You'll never believe the past few weeks I've had."

And if he could talk, I'm pretty sure he would tell me that I did good, and that I was going to do even better. Bas and I had already committed to keeping up my algebra grades, and I was going to make sure I got back on the basketball team and in the ballet recital. I just proved to myself that I could turn my life around. What were a few more extra goals, right?

Oh, and while we were at the ice cream shop, my dad texted asking if I wanted to have lunch with him next weekend. It took me a few minutes, but I messaged him back with a yes. Because I think it's about time I begin saying yes. Yes to becoming a better version of myself. Yes to taking charge of what I want. Yes to bringing people I love into my life.

Yes to it all.

## THE END

# Words from the Author

◆

I was determined to finish this book when 2016 ended because I set a goal for myself to write two books that year. I thought I had finished writing it on December 30, but Treena told me Geri needed an epilogue. So I wrote the last words on December 31, right before I had to rush off to my family parties (yes plural). For that, and for so many, many other things, I thank Treena for always being there for me and my words.

Corinne, to whom this book is dedicated, is my inspiration for Geri. Not because she's also an angry teenager (I don't think she ever was—angry or a teenager haha!), but because when she was in high school, she had two loves: ballet and basketball. And she knew she eventually had to make a choice. Unlike Geri, she chose basketball and that led to years of my family cheering our lungs out at her varsity games. Much more fun than all those years of watching ballet recitals heehee!

Bas practices aikido because I have always been fascinated by the martial art. I still haven't tried it out, but I keep asking Ms. Ada Loredo, my freshman English (and later, MA Literary Criticism) teacher if I can watch her classes. For this story, I watched an Aikido Seminar together with my good friend Christian who explained the moves to me. I really enjoyed it and one day, hope to actually try it out.

Agay pushed me to write this story. She told me about a ballet and karate performance which inspired Geri and Bas's dance in the end. And she came up with the title for this book!

Justine and I were actually doing an online writing course together and I used a lot of the exercises to write scenes for this book. I loved it and I like to believe that I was able to do some things differently because of it.

Jay and Mina are champions of the outline. I resisted at first, but when I made one for this book (a very detailed one at that!), it really helped because I was able to put it on hold for a few days while I worked on the kind of writing that pays the bills—then I jumped right back into the story. Thanks to my outline and to Mina and Jay.

Angel is one of my favorite editors. Why? She makes my words sound so much better. What I love is I learn so much just from her edits! And I hope the next time, I'll be an even better writer because of them.

I've always been a fan of Alysse's work and it's such a joy working with her. So asking her to illustrate my cover was the easiest decision—and one I'm so glad I made.

I'm so happy I have found Miles to make my ebooks look pretty, to help me get them ready for printing locally and on CreateSpace, and to listen to me whenever I need to bounce ideas off someone. I hope she feels the same way about me (though I'm pretty sure this is one-sided haha).

Marc, Addie, and Tammy. Just because they will always be acknowledged in all my books whether they like it or not. (But I'm pretty sure they do.)

# About the Author

✦

**Ines Bautista-Yao** is the author of *One Crazy Summer, What's in your Heart, Only A Kiss, When Sparks Fly, All That Glitters,* and *Someday With You.* She has also written several short stories. Among them are "Plain Vanilla," "A Captured Dream," one of the four short stories in *Sola Musica: Love Notes from a Festival,* "Things I'll Never Say," part of the Summit Books anthology *Coming of Age,* and "Before the Sun Rises," part of the Ateneo University Press anthology *Friend Zones.*

She is the former editor-in-chief of *Candy* and *K-Zone* magazines and a former high school and college English and Literature teacher. She is also a wife and mom who lives in the Philippines with her husband and two little girls.

She posts on Instagram and tweets @inesbyao and her author page is facebook.com/inesbautistayao. Her books are available digitally on Amazon and Buqo.ph. Her website www.inesbautistayao.com will be launched soon.